WHAT

HAPPENED

THIS

SUMMER

WHAT HAPPENED THIS SUMMER

BY PAUL YEE

VANCOUVER   LONDON

Published in 2006 in Canada and Great Britain by
Tradewind Books • www.tradewindbooks.com

Distribution and representation in the UK by
Turnaround • www.turnaround-uk.com

Text copyright © 2006 by Paul Yee
Cover photography © 2006 by Raphael Katz
Book & cover design by Jacqueline Wang

Printed in Canada on Ancient Forest Friendly paper.
2 4 6 8 10 9 7 5 3 1

Cataloguing-in-Publication Data for this book is available from The British Library.

Library and Archives Canada Cataloguing in Publication

Yee, Paul
    What happened this summer / by Paul Yee.

ISBN 1-896580-88-2

    1. Chinese--Canada--Juvenile fiction. 2. Immigrants--Canada--Juvenile
fiction. 3. Chinese Canadian teenagers--Juvenile fiction. 4. Children's
stories, Canadian (English). I. Title.

PS8597.E3W48 2006   jC813'.54   C2006-901886-3

*The publisher thanks the Canada
Council for the Arts for its support.*

 Canada Council **Conseil des Arts**
for the Arts **du Canada**

*The publisher also wishes to thank the Government
of British Columbia for the financial support it
has extended through the book publishing tax credit
program and the British Columbia Arts Council.*

 BRITISH
COLUMBIA
ARTS COUNCIL

*The publisher also acknowledges the financial support of the Government
of Canada through the Book Publishing Industry Development Program
(BPIDP) and the Association for the Export of Canadian Books.*

Dedicated to Nancy and Patrick,
who teach and work with young people.
- P. Y.

CONTENTS:

NEVER GO TO
SCHOOL WITH
A HANGOVER

1

I THOUGHT
LIFE WAS GETTING
BETTER

17

YOU CANNOT
MESS WITH FATE

33

DON'T TRUST
YOUR PARENTS

51

ASTRONAUT DADS
ARE A PAIN
75

WE'RE DATING
WHITE GUYS
99

DEATH SEEMS
TO LINGER
123

READING THIS
NOVEL MADE ME
HAVE SEX
145

WHAT HAPPENED
THIS SUMMER
165

NEVER GO TO SCHOOL WITH A HANGOVER

No more drinking on school nights, I warn myself. Not after last night. My head hurts. The eyes blur. This stomach lurches. These halls aren't wide enough; too many lockers are open. It's an outdoor market of sour lunch smells, the snap and fizzle of soft drinks, girls sitting cross-legged, giggling and eating from dainty boxes. There are too many posters of Hello Kitty, too many Four Fab Kings, too many Japanese and Korean ads. Two guys with greasy hair chase one another, shouting and swearing, their runners squeaking against the floor. *No running in the hall, boys. How many times must I remind you?* This place is stifling, suffocating. I have to get out.

My car, where did I park? Not far, I hope. Thinking hurts. I was late this morning. The lot was full. I ended up on a side street, squinting at the no-parking rules. If I can clear my head, I'll be OK.

I can walk straight. Just watch. I can even run. I used to play basketball for school. First string. At every game, through every quarter, my feet were wings. I'm still good. I'm still great. I'm a razor slicing through the enemy. They trip over their own feet. From the corner of my eye, I see the orange rim, the white net. I have momentum. I fly. I shoot. The ball carves a perfect arc. I rocket up, my fists clenched over my head.

Too bad the team let me go.

The main door clicks. A breeze. Sunshine. I can breathe!

Someone grabs my arm. I ease up and pivot, but the grip is tight, like a vise. It's Vice-Principal McGee. We call him McGay.

"Sir! How are you?" I am always polite. Suddenly my head clears, and everything comes into focus.

"This way, Lincoln Wen."

My last chance for fresh air and freedom vanishes. All the kids watch as I'm led away. They have baby-fat faces with blue eyeliner and lip-gloss. They wear glasses and thin silvery necklaces. Now they think I'm cool. *Thanks, McGay!*

"Sir, it's lunchtime." I want to negotiate, man-to-man, face-to-face, but he shoves me ahead of him down the hallway. His fingers squeeze my arm, but I ignore the pain. McGay is tall and wide. His stomach hangs like a sack of sand over his belt. He lacks class. He wears short-sleeved shirts. You can see the sweat stains under his armpits. People say he was once a cop. People say he never turned in his gun.

"Sir, what's going on?" I ask loudly. "It's lunchtime. We're allowed to go out to eat."

McGay does not answer.

I pull out my cell. "Sir, I'll call the police. You're assaulting me."

He shakes his head. The bags below his eyes sag into punched-out cheeks. "What the hell happened to you?" he mutters. "You used to be such a nice kid."

Who wants to be a nice kid? I'll be any kind of kid I want. "I'm still a nice guy, Mr. McGee."

He ignores me.

In the new wing, the ceiling is lower, and I feel taller, more powerful. The lockers here are painted bright orange. Oh, there's Simon Yu. He used to be my buddy, when I was a nice kid playing basketball, following all the rules. He looks away and starts talking to Jumbo Joyce Koo. They're both losers. Ah, I know where McGay is going. Snake social workers hide in these ant-hole offices. McGay knocks on the door of Mr. Wong, the senior counsellor.

"Come in." Mr. Wong is in shorts, Polo shirt, Nike socks and runners. He looks young but thinks like an old man.

"Sorry to interrupt, Mr. Wong, but Ms. Hasiuk and I would appreciate it if you could have a chat with Mr. Wen."

Is this screwed, or what? This meeting was set up long ago, before McGay grabbed me. Why pretend that it's unarranged?

Wong motions to me to come in and sit down. Behind his desk, he rocks back and forth in a reclining chair. I look away. I'm seasick watching him bob up and down. Every time I see him, I see more forehead, more glow. He's balding. Pretty soon his head will look like the moon. I run my hand through my hair. It's long. It's thick. It's clean. It needs a cut. Mr. Wong is Chinese. He's supposed to understand us.

"Lincoln," he says. "What happened in Ms. Hasiuk's class today?"

I let out a breath. I still feel hungover. In fact, I feel sick. I need fresh air fast. I want to shut my eyes and prop my head against the wall.

"You already know, sir," I mutter. "Why ask me?"

"Want to get my facts straight."

I give him a look of disbelief. "Sir, you think Ms. Hasiuk is lying?"

Wong rolls his eyes. The office is tiny, but Wong has covered all the walls with stupid posters. A hand holds up a condom in order to *BE ON THE SAFE SIDE*. A blonde wearing black lipstick and a tight, short skirt saunters away from her smoker friends to *LEAVE THE CLOUD, JOIN A NEW CROWD*. An African face twists in pain because *RACISM HURTS*. A soccer player stands with one foot on a garbage can to *SAY NO TO DRUGS*. Posters aren't real life. And they don't get more real when they're translated into Chinese. *What a waste!*

Wong can't read them anyway. He's a banana: yellow on the outside, white inside, born over here. He's useless. He's travelled to Hong Kong, not as a tourist, not in search of his roots, but to paddle in the International Dragon Boat Races. That's the extent of his so-called Chinese experience. In his team photo, he's the only Asian face. He can't even speak Chinese. How can we tell him what's really on our minds? This school is fifty percent Chinese, lots of immigrants. We're all part of "new" Toronto, the so-called world-class city. The principal thinks Wong is one of us. He's supposed to help us. *Is this screwed, or what?*

Wong unwraps a sandwich, apple and tetra pack of cranberry juice. Pink meat, green stuff and tomatoes are squashed between brown bread. He opens his mouth wide and takes a bite. My stomach clenches. I swallow the bile. My mouth dries up.

He swallows and sips his juice. He smacks his lips. He's torturing me.

"Will you talk to me?" he asks. "I have simple rules in here. No talk, no walk. You decide how you want to spend your lunch hour."

Go flush your rules down the toilet. I slump into my chair.

Wong slurps the dregs of his drink through the tiny straw. He tosses the box into the garbage bin at my side. The box drops in perfectly, without touching the sides. *Show-off. I can do the same. From farther away, with my eyes closed and with my back to the bin.*

"What was Lisa Yip talking about in class?" he asks.

I really have to get out, before I throw up again. "History, sir. Building the railway. Anti-immigration laws. Riots against the Chinese. Racism today."

"You know this stuff already?"

"Who doesn't? Sir."

"Where did you learn it?"

"Hong Kong, sir."

"What happened in the classroom?"

"Ms. Hasiuk wanted a discussion, sir." Every time I say sir, Mr. Wong winces. He wants us to call him Rick. But the rules say we shouldn't call teachers by their first names.

"A discussion?"

I nod.

"What kind of a discussion?"

He wants me to say more. But the more I speak, the more ammunition he'll have. He wants to shoot me down. On the wall hang yellow, red and green pennants from the dragon-boat races. Wong is the sponsor of our school's team. In the spring, the team sells hot dogs, pizza, doughnuts and ice cream to raise funds. Every week they beg for money. Every week they head down to Lake Ontario to practise. Half the team is white. They look strange crouched aboard the Chinese dragon boats. The other kids are Asian or of mixed race. They're just looking for a free trip to Hong Kong.

•

When Lisa Yip came into Ms. Hasiuk's class, I thought that she was too young and pretty to be a lawyer, a filmmaker and an author—not to mention a human rights activist and university lecturer. Those Chinese who are born here, they have a head start. They know everything except the honest truth about themselves. She looked very stylish: straight hair with highlights, tight shirt, short skirt. She showed photos of Chinese gold miners and cannery workers from a hundred years ago. Everything she told us, we already knew. But she kept trying to get a response from us. The white kids kept quiet, waiting for the Chinese kids to speak.

Lisa Yip glared at me, as if I were to blame. When she had walked into the classroom, kids were gathered around my desk. They wanted to hear all about last night's party. Ms. Hasiuk had to bang her ruler and call for order until the class settled down. That made Lisa Yip think I was a troublemaker.

She wrote on the blackboard. She walked back and forth in front of the class. She used the word *we* over and over. She looked pretty hot. No doubt she could handle tough audiences like us. Finally I put my hand up.

Ms. Hasiuk was so happy she almost clapped her hands. Eagerly she asked, "Yes, Mr. Wen?"

There was a pause. I put on a serious frown and said, "May I be excused?" Then I unfolded myself and stood up.

People snickered.

"No," she said.

Is this screwed, or what? "I really got to go!"

"Well, I really want some student participation."

I couldn't sit down, or she would have won this round. No way I could let that happen. So I turned to Lisa Yip. "What were you saying, Miss?"

She frowned when she heard *Miss*.

"The transcontinental railway," she said.

"Those railway workers were coolies, but you talk about them like they were war heroes."

"They worked hard under horrible conditions."

"Life was worse in China. That's why they left."

"So did they deserve to get less than half the pay of the white workers?" She was toying with me, a beautiful goddess looming over a peasant.

"You told us they did different work from the whites."

"I'm glad you were listening."

"I heard every word. So, if there was no work at home, wasn't it better for them to come here? And the wages here, weren't they better than those in China?" Then I looked to Ms. Hasiuk. "Can I be excused now?"

"Be quick."

It felt good to outwit Ms. Stir-the-Shit and escape the classroom.

In the washroom, I filled the sink with cold water and plunged my face into it several times. Then I lit a cigarette and blew the smoke out the window. But I still felt sick. I thought about sticking my finger down my throat. I didn't want to go back, but I knew if I didn't Ms. Hasiuk would make trouble for me.

When I got back to the classroom, Lisa Yip stopped speaking until I sat down. Then she spoke about redress, about demanding the government refund the head tax collected from early Chinese migrants. "We have to address the wrongs of the past, even if it would be easier to forget them."

Again she embraced the kiss of death by asking the class for questions. "This is a controversial issue. What do you kids think about it?"

No one spoke up, but a couple of kids looked at me. They wanted me to say something. They're all such losers. No guts, no backbone.

She tried again. "Do you think today's taxpayers should pay for the mistakes of earlier generations?"

No takers. She should offer cash. Then people would speak out.

She looked at me. "What about you, Mr. Wen? You have interesting opinions."

I couldn't back down. "If racism is such a big problem, then wouldn't asking the government for money make it worse?"

She nodded curtly, as if impressed. "If we show people that we won't walk away from racism, then maybe they'll think twice before they dare to act racist."

I didn't even realize I was shaking my head.

She cocked an eyebrow at me. "You don't agree?"

I looked away. *Oh no. Not me. I wasn't saying anything else.* It would only lead to more trouble.

"Come on, class, speak up," Ms. Hasiuk said. "These are important issues."

Lisa Yip smiled smugly. "If someone treats you badly because you're Chinese, would you just walk away?"

I raised a fist. "I'm ready to fight."

"Oh no," she said quickly. "Fighting doesn't solve anything."

"At Delaney Junior High," I said, "kids were picking on a Chinese boy. He complained to the teacher. But nothing happened. His parents spoke to the principal. Still nothing happened. Finally the kid packed a baseball bat in his backpack. The next time he got harassed by those bullies, he pulled it out and smashed one guy's knee. No one ever picked on him again."

"Is that a true story?" asked Ms. Hasiuk, her arms crossed over her chest.

I shrugged.

She turned to the class. "Anyone else hear this story?"

Several hands went up. I had to stifle a laugh. I made up that story.

Ms. Hasiuk frowned at me. "You have quite an imagination, Mr. Wen. Hearing a story, or telling a story, doesn't make it true."

"You saying I'm a liar?"

"Just a storyteller, a good one."

•

Wong comes out from behind his desk and sits on it, facing me. "A friend of mine is vice-principal at Delaney. She would have told me about any violent attacks."

"Sir, teachers don't hear everything." That's the truth. Wong should buzz his hair, military style. His bald head wouldn't stand out so much.

"A smashed kneecap? That's major. The police would have been brought in."

I'm backed into a corner. "What's the problem, sir? Do you want me to apologize to Ms. Hasiuk?"

"No, that's not it. I'm talking about when you vomited in front of Lisa Yip."

"I really was sick, sir. I'm still sick."

"Ms. Hasiuk saw you stick a finger into your mouth."

"I never did! I swear I didn't."

"Then tell me what happened."

"Nothing happened."

"Ms. Hasiuk and Mr. McGee think it's time to call in your parents."

"No!" I try to make sure that school life goes smoothly—attendance, marks, meetings, report cards, permission slips. So far there's been no trouble, nothing that would bring in my parents. "I went to a party last night. It went on until really late. When I woke up this morning, I was sick, really sick."

Mr. Wong looks really mad. He holds his teeth together and hisses, "If you were so sick, you should have stayed home from school today. Have you anything more to say?"

"My parents expect me to go to school every day, sick or not."

He looks exasperated. Now he has to say more. He doesn't want to. He doesn't want to scold.

"That's not good enough," he says.

But what else can I tell him—that my father just flew in from Hong Kong last night, that he's been away four months, that I couldn't face him this morning after coming home drunk?

"What happened in class?" Mr. Wong continued.

"Lisa Yip started handing out petitions, sir. She wanted us to go and collect more signatures for redress. You know about redress, sir?"

"Of course I do!"

"Sir, the only people who took the petitions were white kids. Except for Joyce Koo. So Lisa Yip came down my row, putting petitions on every Chinese desk. When she got to me, she put down a big stack."

I don't tell him that she gave me a smug smile.

"I don't know what happened next, sir. I grabbed a few; I ripped them in half and dumped them on the floor.

Then I threw up. I didn't know it was coming. I would have turned away, sir."

Wong's ten fingers make a tent in front of his face. "You know," he says, "in my high-school days, I was the same as you. I didn't know anything about the history of the Chinese over here."

He talks about himself, trying to build rapport, telling me what an idiot he used to be. He had a chance to learn to speak Chinese, but he turned it down. Now he regrets it. Now it's too late. Telling me all this makes him feel better. He thinks we are somehow *brothers*, but he almost puts me to sleep.

I nod. "Can I go now, sir?"

"I don't want Mr. McGee bringing you here again. Understand?"

"Yes sir."

•

Heading out of town, I zip through the traffic and hop onto the 401. If I want, I can drive all the way to Montreal without stopping. The lanes are wide. I step on the gas and soar. Signs with numbers and arrows flash by. I weave through cars and trucks. No one wants to race me. A text message is waiting on my cellphone, but I don't care. Wong was right. I should never have gone to school today. He thinks he knows everything, but he doesn't.

NEVER GO TO SCHOOL WITH A HANGOVER

Teachers don't want real discussions. They don't want to hear what kids think. They want us to hear what *they* think, but they don't know anything. They say they want us to have a good time at school, that they want us to feel like we belong. But then they keep bringing in Lisa Yips, who remind us that we're different.

Teachers should say, "Never go to school with a hangover."

Teachers have no idea how hard we try to fit in. We learn English. We dress like everyone else. We eat pizza and hot dogs. We raise money for the United Way. We cheer on the school teams. We can't fight the racism of the past.

The other day while I was walking through the hallway, a white kid called out, "Hey Wen are you going?"

"Where?" I answered.

The kid looked at his friends, and they all burst out laughing. "Stupid, I wasn't talking to you! I was asking my friends about the time!"

Ha ha. Very funny. Would it have helped if I had said, "We built the railway, you know!"

Is this screwed, or what?

I THOUGHT LIFE WAS GETTING BETTER

"AIMEE! HELP! HAN-MING! HU-LAN! HURRY!"

I've never heard such a loud wail from my mother. My brother bursts from his room, and we dash through the kitchen into the backyard. Ma is kneeling by Ba, who is flat on his back on the grass. His eyes are closed.

"Ba fell out of the tree! Go call an ambulance!"

Han-ming runs into the house.

"I told your father not to prune the apple tree himself!" Ma's hands flap and flutter over his chest. "I told Han-ming to do it, but he paid no attention."

I know there's more to do: Red Cross training at school taught that the first few minutes after an accident are critical. But in my panic I can't recall how to treat a fall victim. I dart into the house and upstairs to Han-ming's room to google the Web for instructions. On the screen, two naked men are kissing, their bodies pressed tightly together.

Repulsed, I retreat from the computer. I grab a blanket from the bed and sprint back outside. My father is trying to sit up. Ma sends Han-ming out front to wait for the paramedics.

The X-rays show my father is okay, but the doctors tell him to stay home for a few days. Next morning Ma won't let him go to church with us. That afternoon, a steady stream of visitors, almost the entire congregation, comes to pray for my father's health. Han-ming disappears as usual, leaving Ma and me to serve everyone tea and cakes. I get stuck washing and drying an unending loop of cups and saucers because we don't have enough to go around.

I feel like hurling the teapot through the window. Just when I thought life was getting better, my brother creates more trouble for our family. He is more bother than he's worth.

On the outside, my family looks normal. We live in a neighbourhood with long, curving streets. We are not rich, but both my parents work, and there is a car in the garage. My brother plays basketball on the school team. Both of us are expected to get good marks and go to university.

Three years ago, we weren't doing so well.

Ba was ready to (a) commit suicide, (b) return to China in humiliation as a failed man or (c) borrow money from everyone he knew to buy five hundred lottery tickets.

Ma was about to (a) divorce Ba, (b) start an affair with our landlord or (c) have a mental breakdown due to severe depression.

I was ready to (a) change my name to Helen Shay, (b) bleach my hair blond or (c) shoplift a pair of $170 jeans.

And my brother was cheating at school and experimenting with drugs.

●

One day three years ago, after five months of living in Toronto, my brother refused to go to school. When the subway train reached our stop, he wouldn't get off.

"I won't go," he said in Putonghua. "I hate that place. I hate all the teachers."

I pulled him to the door, but he grabbed the pole.

"You can't do this," I whispered angrily. "The school will call Ba and Ma."

"Don't care! Let go!"

The warning bell sounded; doors slid shut and the train lurched forward.

I scowled at him. He glared back. We didn't speak. Several stops later he got off, and I followed. He had heard somewhere about tunnels connecting all the downtown office towers. He imagined they resembled Beijing's bombproof tunnels, built for nuclear war. Toronto's passages turned out to be underground shopping malls. Still, Han-ming wanted to explore. First he bought coffee, and then we sat and watched people rushing to work.

"Hungry?" he asked. He threw down two large chocolate bars.

We were both miserable.

"That Mrs. Jiang, I hate her," Han-ming declared.

"Mr. Jiang too," I added.

We were staying with these people Ba knew from Beijing. Mr. Jiang's wife had back pain and never slept. His daughter was thin as a broomstick and never ate. They quarrelled constantly, shouting at each other as if we didn't exist. We couldn't get our own place because Ba wasn't working yet. Mr. Jiang drank a lot, and sometimes he and Ba drank together. Once, when Ma told Ba to stop, he shoved her hard. She fell and banged her head against the corner of the cabinet. Then Ba accused her of flirting with Mr. Jiang, because he coached Ma in English. Ba was right about that. More than once I saw our landlord staring dreamily at her.

That day, as Han-ming and I strolled by the shops, no one paid any attention. Security guards didn't ask why we weren't at school. The malls reminded us of those in Beijing, with gleaming marble floors, wall-sized windows and soft cheerful music. The store displays, the exaggerated poses of the foam dummies and the glittery fashions all looked familiar. In one store, Han-ming tried on Nike runners that were authentic goods, not knock-offs.

Then he told the salesclerk, "I'll buy them."

At the cash register, he handed over eight twenty-dollar bills.

Outside the store, I grabbed him. "Where did you get that money?"

"You don't need to know."

"Tell me!" I shoved my face close to his.

He shook his head.

I felt hurt, because Han-ming had always confided in me before. "Don't buy me chocolate bars with your stolen money!"

He grinned. "Who said I bought them?"

"Ma will see your new shoes. Then what?"

"I'll leave them in my locker at school."

I was sick and tired of covering up for him. When we were still in China, an arcade operator had caught him feeding fake coins into video games and dragged him to the public security office. At home I had seen his stash of metal slugs but hadn't said anything. I also knew he was cheating at school and cutting classes. Again, I hadn't said anything. It was after his teachers called my mother into the principal's office that my parents started seriously talking about emigrating to Canada.

Then I heard a voice call out, "Hu-lan! What are you doing here?"

It was Carmen Zhou from homeroom class. She explained she was cutting through the mall, taking her mother to a downtown doctor. She smiled at us but didn't ask why we weren't in school. Next day, Carmen invited me to church. There, I met her mother again, and the next thing I knew, Mrs. Zhou had found a job for Ma and an apartment for us.

My mother was so happy at seeing our new apartment that she cried while thanking our new friend.

Mrs. Zhou shook her head. "No, don't thank me. We should thank God. Let's pray."

That weekend, my entire family joined her church. In my mind, this was an astounding miracle, because Ba, the scientist, had always scoffed at religion. "Give me proof that God exists," he used to say. "I need concrete evidence of his powers. Otherwise it's all just made-up stories."

At church he met Mr. Guo, who later arranged a laboratory job for him. More importantly, Carmen Zhou volunteered to tutor Han-ming in English. Under her influence, his marks improved. He even started playing basketball again. They became such close friends that I couldn't help but feel a little jealous.

Soon my parents were part of a telephone circle of church parents that was busy every night.

"On the math quiz, what mark did Hu-lan get?"

"For the piano exam, what song is your son playing?"

"You think rollerblading is dangerous?"

"Which math tutor is the best?"

Since joining the church, my parents have become very serious Christians. Last year our pastor asked the congregation to write to their members of parliament, urging them to vote against same-sex marriage. Ba obeyed right away. A list of the entire congregation was posted on the bulletin board, and each family had to tick off its name after sending off a letter. I didn't pay much attention at that time, but now I see why Han-ming began making excuses to avoid church.

●

Today, I lie to Ma about why I have to miss church. I say I have to see an exhibit at the Royal Ontario Museum for biology class. Then I take the subway downtown.

Not long ago, my fellowship group discussed lying. One lie leads to another, we agreed. It pulls you further and further from the truth. But someone said lying is all right if you are protecting someone from harm or if you do not benefit from it. On these counts, I am still a good Christian, since all I'm doing is looking for a new church—one that will accept my brother without condemning his sexual orientation. I found a couple of churches on the Web, and now I need to check them out. If my parents are ever to accept my brother's secret life, then it'll be easier if he's a member of a church.

But I fear breaking another commandment—*Honour thy father and thy mother.* Ba will be furious if Han-ming and I join a different church. He will be shamed in front of all his friends in the telephone circle. I don't know what he might do, and that frightens me.

Above the tracks loom high-rise condos. In their polished walls of glass are reflected wide stretches of dark-grey clouds. I read the cheerful advertisements over the car windows.

If you take this training, there are plenty of jobs.

If you tune in to this radio station, you will have fun.

If you go to this website, you will meet exciting people.

To be born here, to speak English fluently, to be a westerner, how wonderful it must be.

When the train reaches the next station, Shelley Mei steps in and gives me a big smile. We speak Putonghua.

"Going to church?"

I nod. "And you?"

"Math tutor."

"So early?"

"She had no other free time." Shelley frowns. "Why are you on this train? Your church isn't this way."

"I'm looking for a new one."

"What's wrong with your old one?"

"Nothing." I can't tell her the truth. "I want to try something different."

"Where's Han-ming?"

"At home sleeping."

"Hasn't he quit church?"

"No, he's just lazy. He still goes to youth fellowship." But I wonder, does she know about him? She knows all the gossip about the boys.

"He's so different," Shelley says confidently. "From you, that is."

Why is she so friendly all of a sudden? She never talks to me in class. No doubt she's fishing for new gossip to feed her friends.

"You and him are twins, but you're not like him at all," she continues. "You're on the honour roll and he's not. You're quiet, but the basketball team is always getting into trouble. Remember when Lincoln Wen got kicked off the team?"

I open my textbook, but she keeps talking. "So why doesn't your brother have a girlfriend? All the other guys on the team do."

"He still misses Carmen." I have to protect him.

"No way! They weren't dating! They were just friends."

"How would you know?" The Zhous moved to Halifax last summer.

"Carmen told me!"

Her loud voice makes me feel small.

"Is there something wrong with him?" she persists. "All the girls talk about him behind his back." She bends in close. "Everyone on the team has fake ID so that when they go out of town, they visit the bars and get drunk. Did you know that?"

Her eyes catch mine, and I can't look away. She is trying to make me feel stupid. Our church says people shouldn't drink, and Shelley thinks she's caught me being dishonest. People who don't believe can never understand our faith. God fills my heart with warmth and generosity. I am safe under His protection.

"Of course I know," I lie again. "Everyone knows that."

"I heard that when the team played in Montreal, your brother and Hugh Somers went to a gay bar."

"Those guys will do anything for a laugh."

"I hope they didn't dance with one another!" giggles Shelley.

I laugh loudly for effect. "I wish I could have seen that!"

The train slows and stops. Shelley jumps up. "See you tomorrow!"

A second later, the train speeds out of the station. I hate that girl. I hate my brother. Why can't he be normal? Why can't he stop making trouble for me?

My hands are very cold. Shelley has had several boyfriends. She was in the band, so she knew Hugh Somers. He plays lead trumpet and is captain of the basketball team. At first, all the girls were chasing him. Then people learned he was gay. His locker was kicked in and spray-painted with obscene words. The troublemakers beat him. He was taken to hospital. There were rumours of brain damage. Kids wept in the hallway and hugged each other. When he came back in a wheelchair, the school sponsored Human Rights Week. His friends, including Shelley, rallied around him. It is easy to be gay if you are a westerner. Hugh's parents love him so much it doesn't matter if he's gay or not. That's not going to happen in our family. If a Chinese gay person gets beaten up, who will be there to stand up for him?

•

"Hello, and welcome to our church." A middle-aged woman with greying blond hair smiles at me. She must be an usher. "Are you here for the service?"

Behind her, people are entering the church. Women in nice dresses. Girls in long skirts with velvet bows in their hair. Young fathers carrying toddlers. Street people with unkempt hair and blankets wrapped around them. Well-groomed men in couples and groups.

"Wonderful! First time here? Are you from out of town?"

I give the name of our neighbourhood.

"Well," she chuckles, "some people think that is out of town."

"This is a nice church," I say hesitantly.

"One of the oldest in the city. We have a long history."

"Your building looks well taken care of."

She smiles. "We like to think the Lord is helping us." Then she asks, "Do you want to meet our youth group?"

The organ starts playing, and people stream into the church. When the music stops, the minister lifts her arms and welcomes everyone. She sounds happy and strong. That calms me. The first hymn is *All Things Bright and Beautiful*. I know it in Putonghua. It is a good way to practise English, singing from the hymn book. Ba never sang, never mind whether they were Chinese songs or western ones. He used to say singing reminded him of days when people were forced to sing to show their love for the Communist party. Now he walks around the house humming hymns. His favourites are *Crown Him with Many*

Crowns and *Faith of Our Fathers*. He always sings off key. Our home congregation is too polite to tell him how terrible he sounds.

The final line of the hymn makes my knees tremble. "How great is God Almighty, Who has made all things well."

Did God indeed make all things well? If so, then my brother is not a sinner. That means my church is wrong and this church is right. If only our fellowship had discussed these things.

The congregation stands for the call to worship. From the program, I call out responses. They warm me. God is listening to me. He hears me speaking English. When the minister leads a prayer, I bow my head. Another pastor is leading me to God. Will I fit in at this church? I hope Hanming comes to this church with me. A tear slides down my cheek. My head drops, and my hair hides my face.

After *amen*, the minister says, "Let us each pray now, in silence. Let us use our own words to approach God. Let us listen for God's spirit."

O all-powerful and all-loving Heavenly Father, please let my parents be happy. For the sake of their children, they worked hard and bravely immigrated. Please let my brother be happy. My parents may disown him, and then our church and their friends will praise them. My brother needs a safe place. A church like this one. Keep him safe from those who would hurt him.

O Heavenly Father, help me. Jesus said, "Blessed are the peacemakers, for they shall be called sons of God."

Let me be the peacemaker in our family.

O Heavenly Father, let this church protect my brother. Now it is time for me to be strong.

The organ pumps out deep rich music. Congregation members walk up to the pulpit to read from Isaiah, the Psalms and Luke. I hear familiar words, familiar tones of joy. The minister offers a sermon, but my own thoughts crowd out her message.

The offering is taken. When benediction comes, the triumphant bounce of the organ fails to cheer me up. Fresh air will help, I think. And some food.

On my way out, I follow two men in the slow-moving throng. Lines of people from each aisle converge at the grand doors. Then I notice the men in front of me are walking hand in hand. Their hair is neatly trimmed. Their dress pants have sharp creases. One wears a white golf shirt, the other a pink sports shirt. At the men's necks, both shirt collars encounter dark tans. I am curious to see the men's faces. As they reach the grand doors, a man calls from the other line. He is holding hands with another fellow. There are loud words of surprise as the two couples greet each other. Then White Shirt greets the man in the other line with a loving kiss. I whip my face away. Around me, people are smiling. When I turn back, Pink

Shirt is holding hands with another man. I lower my head. Something catches in my throat. It is my brother's name.

I almost call it out, but then I see it isn't him at all. I push by and race out the door. I run down the street, not knowing where I will go. My backpack bangs on my back. At the first corner, I turn and cut the church from my sightline. I run until my breathing fails. I find a bus shelter and sit, panting. I want to go home, run into my room. I want to shut the door, put on my earphones and jack up the music. But my limbs are paralysed.

That kiss made me run like a frightened criminal. I'm no more helpful than our pastor.

When a bus passes by, I look up. It is laden with passengers. The bus glides farther on, toward its next stop. It keeps on going. Soon it cannot be seen.

My cellphone rings. It's my brother. I let the phone ring. He's the last person I can talk to.

I finally stand up. I vow to come back next week.

You Cannot mess with Fate

IN HONG KONG, GOOD BOYS STUDIED HARD AND DIDN'T WASTE MONEY ON FANCY CLOTHES. GOOD GIRLS LISTENED TO THEIR PARENTS AND DIDN'T WEAR MAKEUP. RESPECTABLE BOYS HELPED IN THE FAMILY BUSINESS AND DIDN'T SMOKE. RESPECTABLE GIRLS CAME HOME EARLY AND DIDN'T WEAR SHORT SKIRTS.

Me? I smoked cigarettes. Not every day, just sometimes. At the arcade, I played video games; the bigger the screen and the louder the sound effects, the better. I also played basketball and bought lots of runners. Ba nagged me to cut my hair, because he thought I looked like a girl.

Ba lost hope long ago about me going to college. Once he gave up that idea, he hoped that I would continue working in his shop and later run it. But I only worked there to get money to date girls: naughty ones who enjoyed drinking and nightclubs, studious college types who flirted with me, nice girls so shy you had to pry open their hands and family friends' daughters who pouted at being set up on blind dates. Some of them slept with me, but others refused. No problem: I knew that out there somewhere was a perfect girl who would sleep with me forever.

Then my life took a big detour. Before graduating from high school, I left Hong Kong and came to Vancouver. My English was bad. I had to work as a busboy at the Jade Garden. I was only eighteen and already a father. Worst of all, I had never been in love.

I feel like I'm dreaming, stumbling through someone else's life. I look at the ring on my finger and don't remember anything about my wedding banquet. On my day off, even watching large-screen TV is exhausting. As I lie on the sofa, I shut my eyes, listen to my son cry and think about my life.

•

My father was one of those old-fashioned men. You know, the kind who thinks his life isn't complete if he doesn't have a son. His first wife and children died in China, before Ba came to Hong Kong. His second wife died too, after raising four girls. My father married again and kept trying. When I was finally born in 1987, my father was 57, older than some of my friends' grandfathers. My mother passed away when I was seven, so I've known my father longer than her. He and I were not close. Every morning he wove his long strands of hair into a net to drape over his bald head. It looked pathetic.

Ba liked to smoke and drink with his friends. He liked to gamble and scold and call politicians stupid. When I lived with him, he never complained about doing the chores around the house. After Ma died, at nights he ironed my school uniform and cooked dinner. My sisters bought me cheap clothes from the outdoor markets, but Ba let me buy brand-name goods. That started the girls at school looking at me.

When I started playing basketball, Ba sneered, "Son, you'll never grow tall as those Americans. Thinking of the Olympics? Dream on!"

Everyone at school followed basketball, everyone from the principal to the classics teachers, from the bowlegged janitor to the ladies who hawked hot snacks at the entrance. The TV showed the Asian league, games between China and Korea, the American leagues and college ball. Of course, a betting pool was organized. The first girl I slept with, she attended four games before I noticed her. Her name was Lai-wah.

I was fifteen then, but it was easy meeting girls. It helped that I was tall and athletic in a crowd of shorter kids. And my being the youngest in my family meant that Ba was generous with spending money.

"Make sure you eat your fill at lunch," he would say. "And get a haircut!"

He trusted me.

With Ba running the print shop all day, it was no trouble to bring girls home, you know, to do homework together. Sometimes the weather was so hot and humid that the first thing we did was to take a shower. Some girls were serious about studying, so my essays improved one term when I befriended Lu Sai-fong, the principal's daughter. Ba liked me to have girlfriends: he'd invite them to stay for dinner if he came home when we were still there. Ba had his own woman friend. She phoned our house all the time, but never left her name.

"I'll phone later," she would say in a husky, languid voice. "It's nothing urgent."

I was ten when Britain handed the colony of Hong Kong back to China in 1997. All I remember was a dreary, sodden day with lots of rain. Cannons roared, military bands played and the English flag came down one last time. Some people wept. On TV we saw fireworks, soldiers, crowds cheering. By then, all the people who feared the Communists and who could emigrate had already left for North America, Australia and New Zealand. Nobody wanted to live under a Communist regime.

My father was different. He always said, "I was born a Chinese person, so I belong on Chinese soil. What kind of life could I have in a foreign country?"

I was glad to hear him say that because I only had one home—Hong Kong.

"Hong Kong has its own history, its own way of life," Ba declared. "We worked hard to build up this place. We cannot just hand it over to the Communists."

Life actually got better in the following years. The stock market recovered; real estate prices went up; and former residents moved back to Hong Kong. These ex-immigrants complained loudly: "Oh, the taxes over there are so high! Impossible to start a business! Oh, the market over there is so tough to break into; if you don't know the right people, you're sunk! All the time, you feel second class to the westerners. And life is so boring! The shopping is dated, and restaurant food is so-so."

I was glad my old friends were back on the basketball team. We attended sold-out concerts and met more girls. Things went well until 2003. That spring, SARS, the Severe Acute Respiratory Syndrome, slugged an unsuspecting world. Global panic erupted: travellers blacklisted Hong Kong because guests from one hotel had spread symptoms to faraway places like Toronto and Singapore. Tourists, sailors, business people stopped coming. Stores closed. Everyone wore protective facemasks—on subways, in stores, at performances. In six months, things were under control, but people were still nervous. SARS had originated in China, and Hong Kong people grumbled about the Chinese government not releasing reliable information.

One day when I came home Ba said, "Son, next month we're emigrating."

"Not me!" I shouted.

"Yes, you will!"

"I don't know English!"

"Then you'll learn."

"I don't want to learn!"

"Stupid boy, look around. People are leaving again."

"Others are staying."

"They have no choice."

"What about the print shop?"

"You'll never get rich running that business. It's too small, and we can't afford to buy new presses."

"But I like it."

"After you become a Canadian, you can come back. The least your father can do is to open a door for you."

I begged him to let me stay behind. Third Sister said I could live with her. I talked about needing to graduate from my old school. Ba knew I was lying: that year, my basketball team was about to win the league trophy.

"Son, if you stay, you'll lose a big chance. Once you turn eighteen, you won't qualify as a family immigrant.

Can you live under the Communists, can you stomach the corruption?"

I had just turned sixteen and thought I had lots of time.

Ba reminded me about June 4, 1989, in Beijing's Tiananmen Square, when much civilian blood was shed. Everyone was shocked by the TV images. Hong Kong's people had wept in the streets.

"If China can so easily slaughter its own people," Ba asked, "then what will it do to Hong Kong residents who demand answers around SARS?"

There was no answer to that scary question.

That first year in Vancouver, I slept all day and all night. I awoke, ate and dozed off in front of the TV. I ate lots of instant noodles. I signed up for English classes but quit. I tracked down a few friends, but it was difficult to get together. Everyone was busy working. A few times, we met at the Asian malls in Richmond and played video games. A few times, we tossed a basketball around.

"When will you go to school?" demanded Second Sister. "Hurry and learn English. Get a diploma. The community centre has free classes. Do you know students come from Asia to study English here? This is the best place to learn!"

Luckily, Ba helped me. "Leave Son alone," he said. "What's the hurry?"

Second Sister also nagged Ba to join a club, watch such-and-such a TV program or make friends with so-and-so. Instead, Ba went to coffee shops to meet his old friends.

Second Sister's house was small. She and her husband argued all the time. Their two daughters refused to speak Chinese to Ba, so he decided we should move out. He purchased a townhouse in Burnaby, learned to drive and bought a Honda Civic.

I wasn't happy. My friends found jobs and girlfriends. Sometimes we went drinking and did drugs. I met beautiful girls who would have hit on me had we been in Hong Kong. It was different here. My English was bad, my confidence low and I didn't know how to get around town. I would phone Lai-wah and Sai-fong or chat with them on the Internet, but after a while we drifted apart. All I did was count the days until my citizenship papers would arrive. Then right away I would return to Hong Kong.

One night, Ba asked, "Son, have you thought of marriage?"

"Are you crazy?"

"When I was sixteen, I almost died. Then you wouldn't have been born."

"Better than living here!"

"When the Japanese soldiers occupied Guangzhou, all the residents fled to the countryside, thinking they would be safe. But there was no food. Your grandfather and I returned to the city to see if life would get back to normal. I was your age then. But the moment we came back, soldiers arrested us. Nobody had told us about the curfew. They took us to be executed. Our hands were tied, and a rope went from your grandfather's neck to mine. On the road, people turned away from us. Your grandfather was weeping and wailing. We passed a noodle man. His customers ran off. Then he held out two bowls of noodle soup to the soldiers. They were very hungry and gulped down the food. The soldiers gestured for more. This time the noodle man pointed at our ropes. The soldiers shook their heads. But the noodle man pointed at our ropes again. Then one soldier cut our ropes, and the noodle man refilled their bowls. Your grandfather and I knelt and put our heads on the ground to thank him. His name was Yuen.

"Grandfather said, 'Today you saved the lives of me and my son. We vow before Heaven and Earth to repay you any way we can. No matter in my day or my son's time or my third generation's, we will return a life to you.'

"After the war, I went to Hong Kong. Your grandfather nagged me to find Yuen, who had also fled there. Every New Year, I sent him cakes. Last year, Yuen's granddaughter came to see me. Her family had no chance of immigrating. They had no relatives over here, no professional skills, no money to invest. But she had a daughter the same age as you."

"You want me to marry her?"

"Yuen's daughter and granddaughter are coming to visit. Maybe she's the girl you dream about."

"No."

"Your grandfather made a promise."

"I didn't."

After that, I refused to eat with him. He left food on the table for me. I went to the mall and stayed all day. I played video games and haunted the food court. At home, I stayed in my room, listening to music.

At Christmas, the visitors arrived. I went to dinner but did not dress up, did not cut my hair. Throughout the meal I scowled. No one had much to say. Hardly anyone ate. The mother looked ready to cry. The daughter, Jenny, wasn't any happier, but she wasn't bad looking. Neither of us talked to each other.

Ba arranged a second meeting so that Jenny and I could meet alone. We met at Metrotown mall.

"You have a boyfriend?" I asked.

She nodded.

"His name?"

"Edmund."

"You love him?"

"Yes."

"You sleep with him?"

"That's none of your business."

"In other words, yes."

"And you? Haven't *you* slept with girls?"

"Yes, lots of them."

"Well, I haven't slept with anyone yet."

"Saving yourself for marriage?"

"Yes."

"Then how can you agree to marry me if you love Edmund?"

"Family duty."

"We'd be telling lies. We'd be signing documents falsely. We'd get punished one day."

"Don't lecture me! We're not the first to do it."

"You don't know me. How can you marry me?"

"And you? How can *you* marry me?"

"It's not the same. I don't love someone like you do."

"This is not about me. It's about my family's future."

"And you? Don't you have a future?"

She stared at the ground for moment, then finally spoke. "When my father asked me to do this, he cried. Right in front of me. He tried to stop, but he couldn't. You ever see your father cry?"

"If Edmund cried, would you go back to *him*?"

"Shut up!"

•

She and her mother were supposed to leave the next day and needed a decision.

"I intend to honour my father's promise," Ba said. "If you don't marry the girl, then I will."

The idea of a seventy-six-year-old man marrying a young girl made me want to throw up.

I slammed the door and left the house. I found some buddies to play poker with. All night, we drank and smoked. I felt hot, then cold; hot, then cold. I thought I was sick, or hallucinating or dying. Next morning, I went to the rec centre basketball court. I grabbed a ball, stood at the foul line and looked up at the hoop. Behind the backboard was a huge sky. In the distance were the North Shore mountains. This was a public court, so there was no net.

If the ball went through on my first three tries, then I would follow my father's wish. I bent my knees, raised the ball over my head and shot it.

All three times, the ball dropped through the hoop. The first time I thought it was just chance. The second time I was shocked. On the third shot, I knew right away the ball would go in. It must have been fated. So I gave my consent and we got married.

●

Edmund's friends sent Jenny news about him. He failed the university entrance exams and ended up working in a fast-food chain. He started gambling. Each time Jenny got news of him, she got more and more sullen. She sat in a dark room, smoking cigarettes.

I left her alone. He's her problem, I thought. She left him, so now she has to face the consequences.

One day she broke down in uncontrollable tears. "No one understands me," she moaned. "Friends say I made a stupid mistake. Why am I so depressed when my family is so happy?"

I didn't know what to say to her.

One day, the immigration authorities paid us a surprise visit to see if we were really living together as man and wife. After that, Jenny decided to get pregnant. In a spirited rush, she repainted every room: lime green, pink and sunshine yellow. Now it was my turn to be depressed. No matter what food reached the table, we ate without satisfaction. If we went walking at the malls, we didn't talk. If we watched funny movies, neither of us laughed. It didn't matter who took the garbage out or who tracked dirt into the house. If Ba forgot to bring home the Chinese newspaper, no one cared.

I had to take Jenny to doctors' appointments, watch her belly bulge out gradually and set up the nursery. I moped around the house like a zombie. I couldn't picture myself as a dad. I was only eighteen years old. I missed my carefree life.

Soon Jenny gave birth. The little boy had tiny, perfect hands and legs. I watched her handle him and said, "You are a beautiful mother."

"Our baby is a miracle!"

Both our families beamed with joy.

But when I was alone, I staggered around muttering, "I can't believe I'm a father."

After the baby came, my life was even more of a nightmare. I didn't look like a father. I looked like someone's big brother. I couldn't even hold the baby properly. He cried and kicked when I reached for him. When he cried at nights, I couldn't sleep. And I couldn't stand the smell when I had to change his diapers.

Every day I went to work early, even though I hated it. At the Jade Garden, my shift ended at 2:00 a.m. If the waiters went drinking or gambling afterward, I always joined them. I partied hard and was the last to go home. If my friends wanted to go for an evening of karaoke singing, I went without Jenny.

Eventually, Jenny's family received their immigration papers.

"Your parents and brothers are safe now," I said. "Your duty is done. If you want to go back to Edmund, we can divorce."

She left the room, slamming the door.

"Don't you love him?" I shouted.

She didn't answer.

•

Several months later, Jenny suffered terrible stomach pains. Sometimes she bled on the bathroom floor. At first she said that nothing was wrong—it was just her usual monthly bleeding. But one day she passed out. Luckily she wasn't holding the baby. At the hospital, the specialists ran tests and asked about her family history. Then they told her she had ovarian cancer. Jenny's family quickly rallied around her.

"Don't worry," they cried. "You can fight this disease and win."

"I know someone who survived it."

Jenny withdrew into herself, refusing to see any visitors. She avoided the hospital treatments and rejected the herbal medicines her parents brewed. Then she stopped nursing the baby.

"Sooner or later, we all die," she said. "I am not afraid. I want peace."

One day, I was left alone with the baby. But no matter what I did, he would not stop crying. Jenny had gone to visit her family, and Ba had gone out to buy groceries. I rocked the boy back and forth. I sang to him. I took him outside and swung him around. Several times I checked his diaper. I shoved the bottle into his mouth. Nothing I did would stop his wailing. His face turned redder and redder. His crying grew louder and louder. I was going crazy. I wanted to hit him or give him a good shake. Luckily, Ba came home right then.

I was so angry my entire body trembled. I needed Jenny to be like a TV heroine who confronted her illness and fought back and got a second chance at life. I needed her to get better. I was afraid that if she died, I would be left all alone to raise our son. Worst of all, how would I ever date again, meet girls or marry another woman? What young lady would want to marry a guy with a child?

I secretly phoned Edmund in Hong Kong. "Jenny is dying and wants very much to see you but is afraid you still despise her. Can you forgive her?"

Edmund promised to come, but by the time he arrived at Vancouver airport, Jenny had died.

After the funeral, Edmund and I chatted alone.

"I think Jenny never told you this story, but you should hear it," Edmund said. "When we were dating, the Wong Tai Sin fortune teller looked at Jenny's face and her palm. He took a long time before announcing that our romance had no future."

"You didn't believe him, did you? He just wanted your money."

"The fortune teller said he had even worse news and very gently asked Jenny if she wanted to hear it. I told her to walk away, but she insisted on hearing. The fortune teller told her she would die young."

I swallowed hard. Can these things really be predicted?

Edmund continued, "Then, Jenny was asked to marry you. She thought it over for a long time. Finally, she told me that if her life was going to be short, then she would use it to do as much good as possible. She didn't believe you could mess with fate."

•

Long ago, a noodle vendor saved two lives. Between two families, a debt sprang up. Then a boy throwing a basketball made a life-changing decision. The debt was settled with great pain.

Now, when I look at my son, I hope he will grow up tall and play basketball with me. Maybe someday he will be on the national team for the Olympics. That way he will make his mother proud.

Don't Trust Your Parents

"Still listening to Cui Jian?" Shelley walks into the condo and grins. "He's so ancient!"

Her perfume is heaven, so I pull her close. Her backpack falls to the floor.

"At least he writes his own songs," I murmur.

"You should speak English," she whispers urgently.

"This famous singer," I fling my arms out, "is China's father of rock music!"

I pretend to be the star MC bringing Cui Jian to millions of screaming fans in the Skydome.

"This is Cui Jian's first international tour!" I shout into my microphone. "His songs caused government to fear him! Central government ordered TV station not broadcast his—"

She covers my mouth with her hand. Her hair smells clean and sweet and glistens with purple, lime-green and blue streaks. Ah, a kiss is coming.

"His songs caused **the** government to fear him," she corrects me. "**The** central government ordered **the** TV station not **to** broadcast his shows."

I fall off the stage and break into pieces. "I cannot pass the exam."

"Yes, you will."

"I cannot remember so much things." I deliberately speak bad English because I want her to correct me and hug me.

It works.

"So **many** things," she says.

Yes, this will help me win her soft heart.

"My father went out." I lick her ear. "We can lie down."

She wiggles away. "Or we can study for the TOEFL."

"In a while, in a while."

"I came to work," she says firmly. "Unlike you, I have to pass this exam."

"I must pass too."

"You won't, not with that attitude."

"What attitude?"

Shelley is determined that I succeed. She promises that if I pass the exam, then she will sleep with me.

●

The most difficult part of the TOEFL will be the second section, where we fill in the blanks with correct grammar. In English, small words are big trouble.

Did you find a girlfriend? Not: Did you find girlfriend?

Did you find the money"? Not: Did you find a money?

Did you find people to drive? Not: Did you find a people to drive?

My father pays $500 for tutorials for me. I go on Saturday mornings from 8:30 to noon. The teacher guarantees every student will pass, or they will receive a full refund. I wonder how he can stay in business. There is so much to memorize that I stopped at Blockbuster to rent another brain.

I am not stupid. In Shanghai, my teachers praised me. Song lyrics stuck to me like wet toilet paper. I knew all Cui Jian's music:

Goin' back to that fine old place

Find the old road and go for a race.

I want to go back home. Those songs are my life. Homework has no melody, no backbeat, no energy and, worst of all, no end. Shelley and I exchange worksheets. The teacher says checking other students' work helps.

*There are **few** drinks here. Not: There is **little** drinks here.*

*We don't have **very much** sugar here. Not: We have **little** sugar here.*

*I can have **more** drinks and **more** sugar.*

Rules, rules, rules. **Few** for things you can count. **Little** for things packed in sacks: flour, rice, salt. Who counts things while they talk?

Examples for the listening section of TOEFL are on a CD. It is my turn to ask Shelley the test questions. I say them when the dialogue sample pauses. My English sounds good when I read aloud.

Someone knocks. I walk over to the door and open it.

"Da-ren, how are you?" my mother says, smiling.

What's she doing back in Toronto?

Her hair is cut short with curls. Her earrings are small. As usual, she looks very stylish.

I call to Shelley, "Question 22 is: What does the man mean to say? A. Women never tire of shopping. B. The woman is tired. C. Shopping with the woman was very tiring. D. He has to buy a tire for his wife's car."

Then I answer my mother in English: "I am studying. My friend comes to help me. We are very busy."

She gives me a funny look meaning, *Are you crazy?* Then she comes in and calls out, "I'm Da-ren's mother!"

Good, no suitcases.

Shelley jumps up. "Aunty, so nice to meet you. We're studying for TOEFL."

Mother turns to me. "TOEFL? Didn't you already write that exam?"

"No. I told all this to you."

"Don't let my stupid son slow down your progress," she warns Shelley.

"We both attend the tutorial," volunteers Shelley. "Da-ren studies very hard."

I call out to Shelley. "This is question 23. How does the man feel? A. He is surprised. B. He is disappointed. C. He is resentful. D. He is angry."

"I came to take you out to lunch." She touches Shelley's shoulder. "You must come too."

Shelley turns off the CD and loads her backpack. "No, no," she says in a panic. "I must go."

Mother lets her run out. *Thanks a lot, Mother!*

She checks her makeup in the mirror and says to me in Chinese, "Did I make your friend nervous, or are you two hiding something?"

*I recommend you take a long vacation. Not: I recommend you **to** take a long vacation.*

*There is a stranger standing at the door. Not: There is a stranger **stand** at the door.*

*There is a limit **to** my patience. Not: There is a limit **in** my patience.*

There is no rule. Remember the pattern.

"Hurry, hurry, hurry," she says. "Come eat lunch."

*I'd rather eat at home, not **in** home. And I **would** rather eat alone than with this bitch.* "I have to study."

"I haven't seen you for almost a year. Aren't you happy to see me?"

*You **rob** a bank and **steal** the money. You do not **steal** a bank and **rob** the money.*

"Father has **a** car today," I say to her in English. "Or is it Father has **the** car today?"

"Just call a taxi," she answers in Chinese.

*I want her to **get** out so I can **get** to work. **Get** has many meanings.* "I'm not hungry." I switch back to Chinese.

She goes into the kitchen and peers into the refrigerator. "Nothing here. I'll go buy something and cook lunch for you."

No! Anything but her cooking. I grab the phone and call a taxi.

•

On Sundays the Beautiful China restaurant is especially busy. It is good to see a few tables of white Canadians among the sea of Chinese. Mother flirts with the host. Right away we receive seats. I look around for friends. No luck. Kids are trapped at tables, leafing through magazines, text messaging or chatting on cells, their bodies turned away from their families.

Mother and I are forced to face one another.

"I have my own business now," she says.

In this conversation, she will have to speak both parts. I came to eat.

"It's a bicycle courier firm," she goes on. "The girls I hire come from the countryside. They have strong legs. We pick only the pretty ones, teach them to use cosmetics and deduct the cost of the bikes from their earnings. They're smart and just as clever as the secretaries and receptionists they make deliveries to. And if they meet the boss, they're more likely than boys to get a big tip."

The food arrives at the table. *Ah, much better than bread and sandwich meat.*

Suddenly she speaks English. "Your father, does he have girlfriend?"

Of course. Just yesterday he told me how waiters love to stare at her breasts. Not!

"**A** girlfriend!" I say.

Mother smiles. "Only one?"

"'Does he have **a** girlfriend?'"

"How do I know? I asked you."

I almost shout. "Your sentence was wrong. You should have said, 'Does he have **a** girlfriend?'"

She switches to Chinese. "Your grandmother misses you very much. She told me to give you this." Mother gives me a package.

They are new CDs—the latest releases from Dao Lang, Yang Chen-gang, Chen Hao.

Grandmother bought them? No, Mother must have. She is afraid I might refuse them if I knew they came from her. Good, she knows how I feel about her.

"Not pirated," adds Mother. "Very expensive."

I put them aside. "We download songs from the net now. For free."

She checks her watch, a sleek circle dotted with sparkling gems. "Didn't you receive my letters?" she asks. "You never responded."

"You should phone. No one writes letters nowadays.

"It's always night here when it's day there."

"And weekends?"

"I have to work."

My mother is quick at excuses. China's army doesn't scare her.

"Why didn't you take me back to China with you?" I ask. "You knew I hated it here."

She was the one who was excited about going to Canada. But when things changed for Ba, she left me with him and returned to China. I was ten when Ba first went abroad. He was a doctor sent to learn the new techniques of western medicine. It was Mother who first heard about the exchange program, and she nagged Ba to apply for it.

She bought expensive gifts for Ba to give to his superiors in order to butter them up. She bought cassette tapes for us to learn English. She and Ba learned quickly, but not me.

"How would I have been able to take care of you?" demands Mother. "In my letters I told you. I had no place to live, no job. Your father refused to send money."

Yes, I remember hearing his threat when they were arguing.

Then she says something surprising, "If you still want to return to China, I will arrange it. Next week, you can come back with me."

Of course I want to! I've dreamt about it so many times that I feel I'm already there. I've spent hours imagining Nanjing Road at nighttime. It's a million times busier than Yonge Street. Crowds push in from all directions; neon signs form a flashing canopy overhead; couples walk hand in hand; and security officers hassle the peasant vendors. A baritone sings army songs for spending money, while department stores blast out high-energy music. I hear Pu-tong-hua. I hear Shanghai dialect. Shall I go to Kentucky Fried Chicken or Gou Bu Li for fast food tonight? I am invisible. Everyone is Chinese, like me. I don't feel out of place. I am not trying to balance on a tightrope high above the ground, reaching for a balloon that evades my grasp.

Mother continues. "Come back and you can study, do whatever you want. There are private colleges and training schools. Or I can set you up in a business."

My mind is muddled, giddy. I gesture at the dishes. "Are you eating?"

"The situation is very good now," she says. "New buildings are springing up, people are starting firms, highways are being built. You can buy anything you want. I never imagined things could change so quickly."

I know. I know all this. I chat with my friends over the net. Shanghai has more clubs and rock-and-roll bands than before, plus heavy metal and even jazz. There are concerts at the arena, in small halls, in empty stores. Sometimes you pay, other times you don't. Sometimes the police shut down concerts, but they can't stop the music because the net tells the fans where their favourite musicians will play next. I pour tea to finish the meal.

"Enough?" asks Mother. "Shall I call for more?"

I shake my head.

"I will help you regain your Chinese citizenship," she says.

Of course she remembers. When we arrived, Ba was already a Canadian, and he got me citizenship because I was underage. Mother would have had to wait three years and then take the exam, but she didn't.

"Are we done?" I ask.

"Let's go shopping. I'll buy you some new clothes."

"I buy my own clothes." I stand up.

"Then take this money."

At the other end of the mall is Happy Days Arcade. I park my tokens at the newer machines. I log on and chase the Sorcerer Stone that Dr. Doom has stolen. I play this game so often that my moves are instinctive and accurate. I know when to expect Venom, when to kick, when to punch, when to jump, when to swing. When Armoured Fortress appears, I know to jump, dodge and shoot. Glancing up, I see Xie Han-ming on Dance Dance Revolution, bouncing and twisting on the dance board like a puppet high on drugs. He's a strange one: always by himself, even though he's on the basketball team. I look away. People say he might be gay.

I should be jumping up and down with joy. I can throw my English language books out the window. I should be phoning Leon and Ming and laughing while they gnash their teeth with envy. I am dancing atop the CN Tower. My dream has come true. The door to the prison has swung wide open. But here I am, perched in the dark, watching the stars flash by on the screen in front of me.

I'm not having doubts, am I? I would be crazy not to go back. I am about to fail the TOEFL. Shelley will pass, of course, and everyone will congratulate her.

They'll say, "Better luck next time."

And the next, and the next, and the next.

They'll say, "The more times you try, the better you get."

I will be an eighty-year-old writing the TOEFL. They'll say, "Don't lose hope."

I'll lose my mind.

I wonder what it will be like living with Mother. She was a heartless slave-driver. So what if she is rich now? I won't let her barge into my life and act as if nothing has changed between us.

The day she left us, I came home late from school. The condo was quiet, dim. I grabbed some food from the fridge and went to the TV. Ba came out from his bedroom. I sat up and lowered the volume.

"Your mother has gone back," he said in Chinese.

No surprise to me. "You let her go?"

"Couldn't force her to stay."

Of course not. Mother had backbone. Whatever she decided, she did. Sullenly I pointed out, "You're forcing *me* to stay."

He switched to English. "You are still young. You can learn English."

I had heard this too many times. I was forced to swallow it as if it were nutritious, but all it did was make me want to vomit. "Oh yes. I will learn English. I will be a news broadcaster. I will be so good that the government will send me to China to teach English!"

"Just study hard."

"I do!" I shouted in Chinese. "I can't study any harder. Computers won't help! Tutorials won't help! Learning English is not like doing mathematics."

"You must concentrate."

Ba believed that hard work solved every problem. That was his password to success. As for me, whenever I opened a book, I thought of a coffin cover.

He went on, "Your mother and I worked hard so you could have this opportunity."

Time to surrender. Could any teenager survive such pressure? I retreated to my room and dived into Cui Jian's music.

•

At home, Ba sits on the sofa. His feet are on the coffee table. My textbooks are still spread over the dining table. I hope Ba saw them and was impressed.

"Have you decided?" he asks. He is watching *That Seventies Show*. Why does he bother? The jokes are hard to understand. "Your mother phoned me."

Ba speaks only English with me in order to help me learn faster.

"Of course I want to go."

"Go, then. You are old enough to think for yourself."

I wait. There is more coming. There is always more. Doctors want people to listen to them. In China, people looked up to Ba because he had the power to defeat death and bad breath. My friends used to think I was lucky, being the son of a doctor. But medicine always tastes bad.

"If you leave," he says, "you go back as failure."

"**A** failure. I go back as **a** failure."

"You go back as *a* failure. You enjoy that, huh? Your friends, behind your back, they will laugh at you. They will say you could not master English, could not pass the TOEFL. That is why you came crawling back to China."

I explode in Chinese. "You don't know a single one of my friends."

"That is truth," Ba replies in English.

"Lots of people have gone back," I say in Chinese.

"Many stay here," he snaps. "Think clearly before you act. Here the air is cleaner. Parks have grass. At Niagara Falls you can cross the border into America without any problems. Soldiers cannot stop you on the street. People will say you are not only stupid, but you have no long-term vision. You cannot see that your own children's lives will be better here."

In my room, I turn on the music, loud. I can't stand listening to my father. When I speak to him, it is as if I am under water. He has no idea how difficult my life is.

He is deaf to everything but his own thoughts. He too is a failure, a bigger failure than me. That's why he cannot go back to China. The medical authorities here would not certify him as a doctor. He had to retrain as a nurse. When Mother and I arrived two years ago, Ba had four pairs of white Nikes (authentic goods) lined up by the door.

Mother saw them and laughed, "What are these for? Exercising? You don't look in very good shape to me."

•

Next morning when I pull Shelley away from her friends, she comes eagerly. I take her outside to share my news. She'll be happy, because she knows I hate being here. She'll jump into my arms and hug me tightly. She knows learning English has been very difficult for me. Some people have a talent for languages—others do not. That is why we have engineers.

She asks what I think is a tender question. "When do you leave?"

When she looks up, I see tears in her eyes.

"I thought you liked me," she says. Her voice trembles.

"I do, I like you a lot. I would do anything for you."

"Then why are you going?"

"Because I will fail TOEFL."

"I am going to help you until you pass."

"I can never pass."

She stamps her foot. "That stupid exam! Why does it matter so much to you?"

Wait a minute. What is going on? Shelley has never shown such deep feelings for me. We are friends, good friends. We are in the same chat room. We talk at all hours and late into the night. But she refuses to sleep with me. We are not boyfriend-girlfriend.

Shelley is naturally smart and studies hard. She'll be a success even with her rainbow-coloured hair. She belongs here with all the newcomers who believe North America is paradise.

She hurries away. I run after her. "Shelley, I did not know you liked me so much."

"I thought I knew you."

"No, I am very simple, very stupid. Why would you want someone like me?"

She stops, turns around, and I can see she is angry. "You worship Cui Jian and rock and roll, but where does rock and roll come from? You wear Nikes, but where are they designed? You use email, but whose alphabet do you use to get to the Chinese words?"

"Things are changing," I counter. "Soon China will produce more engineers and scientists than America. Chinese technology will surpass theirs."

"China relies on America to buy its exports," she sneers.

"You are ashamed of China."

"You're lazy," she replies. "You are stupid and don't know how to study."

"You are angry because I am dumping you."

She gasps.

I cannot believe I said that. Those words, where did they come from?

•

When I share my good news with Leon and Ming, they hoot and yell as if we are playing drinking games.

"You can smoke wherever you go."

"You'll earn tons of money."

"Think of me when you're revving up at the go-kart centre."

A lot of kids speak English worse than me. When the teacher asks a question, they can't answer it out loud. The teacher asks them to stay after class in order to give them extra help. I feel sorry for them. If someone like me, who is almost ready to write TOEFL, is giving up, then what kind of a future will they have here? Many of them want to go back to China, like Leon and Ming. But they would never dare to challenge their parents. They are cowards. They think they're free here, but they can't speak their own opinions. They think big opportunities await them here. But as soon an employer hears their fractured, accented English, they'll be dismissed like yesterday's fish.

Mother said I should visit my teachers and my principal and thank them for their help. *No, thank you! Teachers don't really care.*

In honour of my good news, Ming and Leon decide to skip classes, and we head to a café for bubble tea.

At home, I quietly let myself in. I think Ba is still on night shift, so he's probably sleeping. I close the door to my room, turn on my computer and put my headphones on. *Ah, my Shanghai buddies are catching up to the news.*

Zhao-shen writes, "Excellent! You're coming back. It'll be great to have more friends here. You'll be surprised how much the city has changed. You better learn to run fast. The girls here like to chase guys. Hope you can help me with my English."

Jing-dan writes, "You're returning at the best possible time. The Olympics are coming to China. People are counting down, day by day. All kinds of really *cool* events are going to be happening. Will you work as an English teacher here?"

Shi-cong writes, "Welcome back! Looking forward to seeing you. Only my sister is sad because she was hoping to visit you there. She and her friends practise English 24/7."

Shou-lei writes, "Ha ha, and you thought you'd escaped writing the middle-school exams. Will you have to take them now? Even if you do, they're not so bad. You'll pass easily. You should score at least 99%."

I miss my pals!

I spin my chair around and survey the room. Should I take my guitar? I never learned all the chords. I'll need several power adaptors for my computer hardware. I'll bring my magazines along and give them to Shi-cong's sister. My clothes I can dump; there's nothing new. I'll give Leon my old CDs. I need a new suitcase. I better phone Mother. I want to buy gifts for my pals. Her hotel number is on the board in the kitchen.

When I open my door, the door to Ba's room also opens. Mother steps out. She is a mass of pale flesh, naked. We both yelp, turn and slam doors behind us.

I start giggling and can't stop laughing.

•

This is my first visit to Ba's workplace, a nursing home for old people. He is the nursing supervisor. The building is an apartment block, surrounded by large lawns with many trees. Pearson International Airport isn't far away, and the drone of planes can be heard. I imagine myself on an airplane flying to Shanghai already. Inside, the home smells of antiseptic. Staff members hurry by with trays of medications and juice on metal trolleys that rumble and clank. One worker hums in a rich, deep voice as she pushes a wheelchair.

"Hey, Ronnie," she calls, "you're early! Can't you get enough of this place?"

"Ronnie?" I chortle.

Ba's name is Ruo-neng. He said he would keep his Chinese name, no matter what. He glares at me.

"Rosa, I worry you are stealing my job," Ba says. His joke falls flat, so he adds, "We're going to Miss Carr's office. Rosa, this is my wife Jian-xi and my son Da-ren."

We exchange greetings. At the elevator, I nudge my father. "What does your name tag say?"

"Don't be rude," he snaps.

"Interesting name!" I say. "Reminds me of that famous general, Dong-bi Wu."

All I can think about is escaping to China.

The elevator door opens. A grey-haired nurse with a firm jaw, sensible glasses and a bundle of files is there.

"Hi Ronnie. Aren't you on afternoons this week?"

"Hullo, Cora," says Ba. "Miss Carr wants meet my family."

He introduces us and we shake hands. Cora turns to Ba. "Mrs. Stone is worse. Another stroke hit her last night."

"Should we keep her here?"

"If the doctor asked me, I'd say she should go to the hospital."

"You want me see her?"

To see her, I think to myself.

"Could you?"

The door opens and she leaves. Ba calls out, "I will see you before I leave."

"Thanks, Ronnie."

I imitate her voice. "Thanks, Ronnie."

Ba ignores me.

Miss Carr has thick brown hair that is pinned behind her head. She's wearing a power business suit. I feel nervous because I want to make a good impression. It will be my goodbye gift to Ba.

She comes out from behind her desk to greet us. When she stands up, she is even taller than I thought. "A pleasure to meet you, Mrs. Zhao," she says. "At our Christmas party, I asked Ronnie why you hadn't come, and he said you were visiting your mother in China."

Mother nods like a bobble-head doll. Her English is worse than Ba's.

Miss Carr turns to me. "And you, young man, you were too busy studying to come to the party."

"Yes, that is true," I say in my best English. "Ba says I must set firm priorities in life. Like always wash my hands."

She smiles. "Yes, that's important here. Your father works far too hard. I'm always telling him to relax."

"Yes," I say, "Doctors say people live longer if they can relax." Then I add, "My father should join the circus. He is too tense."

Miss Carr catches my gaze, then throws her head back and breaks into loud laughter. My parents look anxious, as if I've behaved shamefully. They don't understand puns. I don't either, but someone else told this one in class.

"He was studying for TOEFL," Ba says.

"What will you study at university, Darren?"

Linguistics, I want to say, so I can teach my father how to speak properly. Instead, I shrug. "I do not know yet. Computer Science, maybe."

"Ah yes, I.T. is the way of the future. Your father has been helping people here use computers."

"We better go now," says Ba. "You are very busy."

"Well, very nice to meet you, Darren and you too, Mrs. Zhao. Will I see you at this year's Christmas party?"

Shake hands; smile some more. Time to go wash our hands.

In the elevator, Ba asks, "Do you want to meet the people I take care of? Many of them ask if I have family."

"No time," says Mother. "I need to make phone calls."

"Use my cell," Ba says.

"Can't, my files are at the hotel."

She is itching to leave. I think she may be afraid that if I see more of Ba's world, I will change my mind. Of course, Ba has brought me here for that exact reason, hoping that miraculously I will see him in a new light and then decide to stay. No such luck. Yes, Ba is helping old people live with less pain, but I don't want to stay here a minute longer.

Mother and I go downtown, and I spend the afternoon spending her money on my buddies. I take the longest time looking for a gift for Shelley.

Next morning, I wake up late. I don't have to go to school anymore. I stumble to the fridge to look for food. I hear Ba behind me. He coughs and clears his throat. He looks at me and tilts his head at my new suitcase and the bags of gifts left on the sofa. "I hope you have a receipt for those things. Your mother changed her mind."

No!

I see a letter to me in Chinese on the kitchen table.

> *Son, your English is excellent. I was wrong to*
> *suggest taking you away from your studies.*
> *Listen to me, no matter where you go, you*
> *will go further if you know English. Even in*
> *China, that's true. Your father and I will pay*
> *your tuition no matter what university you*

choose to attend. Your mother truly loves
you. Look to the future and make it as bright
as you can.

I look toward Ba's bedroom. He shakes his head.

I slump into a chair, put my arms on the table and cradle my head.

Mother has destroyed my life. She has no idea. I had a great thing going with Shelley until she came along.

Well, at least now I know. That girl likes me more than I had thought. That's a bonus.

What next?

I have to call her. What should I say besides I'm sorry, I'm sorry.

Never ever trust your parents' words.

No, bad grammar. It should be, *Never trust your parents' words.*

Teachers say shorter is better. It should be, *Don't trust your parents.*

ASTRONAUT DADS
ARE A PAIN

THIS IS MY FAMILY, PUTTING ON ITS BEST FACE, SITTING AT A ROUND TABLE AT THE RUBY PALACE, WAITING FOR THE BEST CHINESE FOOD IN MARKHAM. ACROSS THE TABLE ARE MY COUSINS. YOU WOULD NEVER GUESS THEY ARE TOP STUDENTS AT UNIVERSITY. THE VOLUPTUOUS ONE WEARS ENOUGH MAKE-UP TO PASS AS A HOOKER. THE ANOREXIC ONE IS SO PALE HER SKIN LOOKS FROZEN BLUE. BOTH ARE IN SCIENCE, AIMING FOR MEDICAL SCHOOL. RIGHT NOW THEY'RE BORED, EVEN AS THEY FLIP GLOSSY PAGES OF THE LATEST *COSMOPOLITAN*, CHINESE EDITION. WE HAVEN'T TALKED IN YEARS.

My brother, Homer, is yakking on his cell. Last summer he practically stapled his lips shut and lost thirty pounds. Now he has cool sunglasses, a large circle of friends and a girlfriend. He even signed up for Outward Bound. Ma signed the form without knowing how tough the program is. Since then, Homer hasn't spoken to me because I bet money he would crash on the trek. I'm enjoying the break.

He and I aren't allowed to read at the table; instead, we're told to join the adult conversation. It's supposed to help us mature faster. Ma would ban cells, but she carries one herself. In younger days, Homer couldn't bring his Game Boy even when the restaurant was a zoo buzzing with clicks and pings.

Next to my cousin sits Grandmother, straight-backed and still. She has an elegant face and glistening white hair, but when I photographed her last week she hid her wrinkles and spots behind a fortress of make-up. I almost didn't recognize her.

Grandfather is deaf now and avoids talking. He refused to let me photograph him, but I suspect that if Homer had asked, Grandfather would have said yes. He likes boys better, even though he would never admit it.

I see Simon Yu on the other side of the restaurant with his family. We'll make sure our paths don't cross tonight. It's too embarrassing when parents meet and chat and put down their own kids to make the other couple look better. When I look around, I see interesting faces at all the tables. But I hide my camera among company. It's so annoying when people play shy.

"Oh no, I'm too old."

"Oh no, so-and-so is much prettier. Take her picture."

"Oh no, why waste your film?"

What they really want is a portrait showing them successful and contented. They want pictorial proof that they've conquered every obstacle in life.

Elder Uncle and Aunty are retired teachers. They follow the news in English and Chinese and have opinions on everything. Elder Aunty likes to challenge my father on politics. But it's all talk because neither of them listens to the other.

"Ah, Taiwanese independence. It's a big waste of time," Ba loudly bullies her. "China will never allow it to happen."

Aunty, on the other hand, is soft. "America hates Communism. America won't sacrifice Taiwan to its worst enemy. It could never live down such a betrayal."

"The day that China gives Taiwan independence," Ba snorts, making one of his grand pronouncements, "that's the day war will end forever all around the world."

Second Uncle is an auditor at Toronto city hall and a devoted fan of European soccer. He checks the latest scores on his Blackberry. Second Aunt's face is painted porcelain. She would love for me to shoot pictures of her, but I don't like her. Their kids are away on European internships, so now Aunt and Uncle have nothing to complain about.

The cold platter arrives, and everyone selects a choice piece for his or her neighbour. Teapots swing by, and cups get refilled. The most lethal drink at our table is ginger ale. Ba and his brothers love good Scotch but won't drink in front of their parents.

Ba brags about work. "They all said I couldn't get in on this deal. They laughed at me for trying. 'Way out of your league,' they advised. 'Mouse chasing a cat.' They each bet a thousand dollars I would get squeezed out. Later, I was the one laughing at them."

"Julia, your graduation ceremony, when is it?" Elder Aunty calls out.

"Next week," I answer.

Ba flew in from Taipei to attend. He should fly out before we all remember what a jerk he is. Astronaut dads are a pain.

"Take lots of photos for me."

"Remember Liu Rong-wen, the general's son from Tai-nan?" Ba mentions his old friend. "His daughter is graduating too. He's so out-of-touch he doesn't realize how stupid she is. He's pushing her to become a doctor. He's dreaming!"

"Choose a university yet?" Elder Aunty asks.

I suddenly find the tripe very tough and begin serious chewing.

"New York," I mumble.

"Columbia?"

Thoughts in my head crash and rebound, then spin off to distant galaxies. "College of Art."

I cheat by using the Chinese term for university.

"College of Art?" Elder Aunty looks at my parents. "Not so, is it?"

"This braised pork is dry," I say.

Homer carefully parks his chopsticks. My cousins are discussing today's jellyfish.

"Daughter hasn't told us anything." Ba frowns. "She's still waiting for acceptance letters."

I don't want to tell them that my acceptance letter arrived this morning.

"Some have come," Ma says quietly. She phoned my father in Taipei each time one arrived.

"College of Art?" says Elder Aunty, as if it were an X-rated movie. "I didn't know you had artistic talent."

"It's a three-year program for photography." I am suddenly jaunty. I didn't expect to talk about it so easily, but here Ba can't strangle me. Plus he'll have time to calm down.

"You want to open your own shop?" asks Aunty.

"The day Daughter gets a photo on a magazine cover," Ba sneers, "that'll be the day I send her to art school."

My eyes steer clear of him. "First of all, I want to travel. Maybe work for a news agency."

Fortunately, Second Uncle changes the topic. "Did Ah-Jing buy the house in Hualien?" he asks Ba.

And they're off again, hot on the money trail. Ah-Jing is their other brother, the one who stayed behind in Taiwan. Every adult in our circle has an opinion about real estate there. Are prices going up or down? Is it best to buy now or later? Which development is a better buy?

As for me, I'm thinking this is my last supper. I should feast tonight. I'm Julia the traitor. The one who will be disowned, cut out of the family, disinherited like a criminal. Everything is up to Ba. If he doesn't pay my tuition, I'll be waiting tables all my life.

When we get back home, my parents head straight for their bedroom. Ba arrived two days ago. Mostly he's been sleeping, but it can't be jet lag because Ba doesn't believe in it. As soon as he gets off the airplane, he's on local time. He always complains about the trip taking more than twenty-four hours each way, but it's not that he's stuck in the air all that time. It's waiting for the connecting flight in Vancouver.

Ma stayed home from the shop. So they probably had lots of sex—unless Ba has taken a mistress over there. That would be stupid because Ma takes care of herself and looks good. At the mall, men eye her when she walks by. Sometimes I'm jealous; other times I don't care.

Astronaut Dads Are a pain

In the family room, I lie in front of the TV. Homer is up in his room, plugged into one of his chat rooms. Sometimes it feels like he's cut himself off from the family. At least Ma and I watch TV together. *Buffy the Vampire Slayer* fills the forty-two-inch screen. The show is like kung-fu TV from Asia, only more bizarre. It's cool that her father isn't around. That way, she gets to do what she wants. Now her Mum is lying sick in a hospital bed, and a creature from outer space appears.

Ba is shouting at Ma. Every time he comes back, he rips into her big-time.

"How could you let me lose so much face in front of my brothers! You don't even know what your own children are doing! How do you run this family? Don't you ever think things through?"

She absorbs it like a punching bag. Ba is boss. He was the one who decided we would emigrate, even though Ma's English was pitiful. He picked Toronto, even though Ma had plenty of relatives in Vancouver. Ma wanted to live close to the subway, but the house Ba chose meant she had to learn to drive. Ma begged Ba to attend parent-teacher meetings, but he never came. Bastard. She had to memorize every question, muttering them over and over like Buddhist chants. Ma hated those teacher meetings. No wonder Homer and I studied hard.

I hear Ba yelling.

"Didn't you know about the college of art? Didn't you see her using my camera? Didn't you talk to her teachers?"

I rush upstairs. Ma drops her hands from her eyes. She's been crying. Ba's face is red and bloated, as if from drinking.

"Don't yell at Ma," I blurt out. "Whatever she told me to do, I did. I went to school. I listened to the teachers. The universities, they accepted me. But I changed my mind. Ma didn't change it for me. Art school is what I want. Do you understand?"

Ba goes to shut the door. "We're your parents. Understand that? We just want what's best for you." He sounds like a TV soap opera.

"You think I don't want that too?" Now *I* sound like a soap opera.

"What do you know? You think you're smart? You've seen the world?" His hand flies up to hit me.

Whoa. We're turning into a kung-fu series. We stare each other down. Now we're a cop movie, guns at each other's heads.

"Stupid girl," he hisses, "have you thought this through clearly?"

"Getting into art school, you think it's easy?"

"You think taking pictures is easy? You think you'll be famous?"

"I never said it was easy."

He stalks away, kicking the carpet. "I don't care, I really don't care. The key is this: Can you earn a living at it? I want you to have good clothes to wear and lots to eat. I don't want you to suffer like your Ma and I. And you don't want to depend on a husband."

He likes to throw around tidbits of high drama.

"You think I don't want the same things?"

"Can you raise a family? We can't protect you all your life. You want to go on welfare?"

I bolt from the room, and Ba shouts, "The day Daughter opens her own photo studio, that'll be the day people elect me to run this country."

Ma doesn't say a word, doesn't even move. I didn't expect her to.

I see on my cell that Jeffrey has left a text message. I don't bother with it. Instead, I head back to Buffy, only this time I plug in a cord and clamp the headphones over my ears.

•

A lot of Chinese people don't like Toronto's old Chinatown. My parents don't. They complain it stinks, especially in the summer, and isn't clean enough. I think it's changing. More and more people speak Mandarin there now. Ma shops at the sleek new malls far from downtown. She has friends who work downtown, and they go to Chinatown only because lunch is cheap there. They all complain, sometimes quietly, sometimes deliberately loudly.

"So dirty."

"Too many people. Too many cars."

"Parking is so inconvenient."

"The Vietnamese are running everything."

The attraction of suburban malls is that parking is free, outdoors and safe. There is air conditioning. All year round, it's "twinkle, twinkle, little star." The worst thing about Chinatown is that the food is only so-so.

Me? I like going to Chinatown, even though you can get the same stuff at our local malls. People at school think I'm weird: they think I connect to Chinatown as a mystic link to community and history. The first Chinese settled in Toronto over a hundred years ago, close to Union Station. Everyone pictures Chinatown as a hell with low wages, long hours and bad haircuts where all immigrants pass through. Produce spills onto the street; nylon grannies hawk green onions; and foreign tourists and hard-faced Mainlanders jostle for low prices. Pairs of cops patrol regularly, as if the coarse shouting, the traffic jams and the smells of rotting fruit might suddenly turn ugly and explode like a freakish nuclear bomb.

It's warm today, with clouds in the sky, but not too dark—excellent for taking pictures with black-and-white film. On days like this the light is very soft, and you can record an amazing range of greys, blacks and whites. The camera is special this way. It accepts the world's colours and textures honestly. It's not like the human eye, censoring everything for safe consumption, shutting out the ugly miseries that we don't want to see. Under this even light, the camera captures every wrinkle, every spot and every hair on your face. It shows a truth you can't find anywhere else.

The Golden Castle Bakery-Café is busy. Customers with bulky shopping bags besiege the counter like soldiers massed before an enemy castle. There's no take-a-number system. People are patient, except for grannies, who assume their age trumps all. If anyone scolds them, they're suddenly half-blind or totally deaf. The café is full. It's the mid-morning break for Chinatown workers. I see Uncle Foon. He's not related to me, he's just someone I met while working on my portfolio. He waves. He looks like Grandfather, but he speaks good English, even though it's not perfect. He's sitting with K.S. Tang, the art collector and gallery owner. As usual, K.S. is very fashionably dressed, even wearing a hat. K.S. frowns and, without even greeting me, announces, "This old fool won't go to the opening of his own show."

"Why not?" I ask.

Uncle Foon shrugs.

"You've gone crazy," I mutter.

He has stuffed his mouth full of bread, so K.S. adds, "He says he wants his photographs to speak for him. He doesn't want to come between them and the viewers."

I understand. That's an artist talking. K.S. has no time for that. K.S. the businessman has invested a lot in this event, much more than I have. He invited the mayor, Miss Chinatown, the Consul General and other politicians to the opening. The gallery will be crowded with lights, TV cameras, press cameras, cameras from the Chinese Photo Club—of which K.S. is the president—and idiot-proof box cameras carried by guests. If the artist doesn't show up, K.S. will lose face.

He scowls at me. "Talk to him."

"You know it's not easy to change his mind."

"You're responsible too."

"The exhibition was your idea."

"You're the one who showed me his photos. I didn't even know he was alive or living here."

I won't push Uncle Foon around. I owe him big-time. He took me to places in Chinatown that a girl would never have been allowed to photograph: restaurant kitchens, sewing factories, private clubs, pungent warehouses. Without him, I never would have assembled a portfolio, never would have gained admission to art school.

Uncle Foon points his thumb at me. "The first time I saw this girl, she was standing on the sidewalk being scolded. Old Chow at the hardware store was shouting at her, cursing her parents and ancestors for taking his picture. I said to myself, 'That's not right, such a pretty girl being treated like a child.' Everyone knows what a foul temper Old Chow has. People were crowded around listening to Old Chow yell at her."

"Is that how you two met?" asks K.S.

"Hey, I pointed to my camera, and that Old Chow nodded. I assumed he agreed to be photographed. Why would he get so bothered?"

"Tonight the Lung Gong association honours its ancestors," says Uncle Foon. "Want to come?"

I shake my head. Chinatown I like, but not the banquets. At one gathering, I wasted an entire evening and three rolls of film. People stood like cardboard, flat and shiny, stuck to groups of VIPs. No one stood alone. A person by himself looks totally different from when he's standing in a group. Uncle Foon is an executive of his same-village club. He's always representing it to other organizations. I can tell he's good at unprepared speeches, even though I don't understand his Cantonese or village dialects.

K.S. leans forward and speaks sincerely. "Generations of Chinese know your photographs. They are famous all around the world. No one else documented the war years like you did. People think you're long dead. That's why you must come to the opening."

"Are you going to the banquet early to play mah-jongg?" I ask Uncle Foon.

He looks around the coffee shop. "It's time. Ready to go?"

"Can we cancel?"

"What's the matter? You shy?"

"No!" I look away. "I don't need to shoot anymore. I'm not going to art school."

"The school refused you?"

"No."

"What's the problem?"

"Father won't let me go."

I'm pleased when K.S. and Uncle Foon curse my father. But then I feel disloyal, traitorous. He's still my father, and these men have never met him.

"Let's go take pictures," I say to Uncle Foon. "We can't keep the lady waiting."

K.S. is mystified. "Which lady?"

"A rich businesswoman," Uncle Foon says gruffly.

"I know everyone," says K.S.

"Every hooker too?"

As I follow Uncle Foon, K.S. points to the old man and mouths a silent command, "Talk to him!"

I owe K.S. a favour too. He wrote a letter of recommendation for my application to art school. He said he was very interested in showing my work at his gallery.

On the street, Uncle Foon looks at me. "Want to take pictures or not?"

I shake my head.

"Then why did you come?"

"We had an appointment."

"Going home?"

"K.S. wants me to talk to you."

"Can't you work part time and attend art school at the same time?"

"New York is very expensive."

"Isn't there scholarship money?"

"No."

"What does your mother say?"

Enough of this dead-end topic. I need to get out. But I don't feel like going home. I force myself to be cheerful. "Hey, Old Man, what can I do to get you to the opening?"

"Not a thing."

"I'll come to your house, pick you up and drop you off later."

"You have a licence?"

I feel small admitting that it's only a learner's.

"If I need a driver, I'll call a taxi."

Seniors can be so stubborn, so ungrateful. They argue just to be difficult, just to show you their age makes them superior to you.

●

My mother's store, Fashion Delight, is in Scarborough's Lotus Plaza between a jewellery store and an art supply shop. I'm fetching her because Ba took her car. Business slowed down this year, so she fired her clerk and tries to do everything herself. I'm supposed to help, but I don't care for retail or her line of fashion. Ma turns off the lights as soon as she spots me.

"We have to buy groceries," she says. Dark pouches lie under her eyes. She doesn't like to cook, hates planning menus and never gets the right balance of textures from dish to dish. But because Ba is here, she has to play supermom.

We walk towards the supermarket at the far end of the mall. All last week, before Ba got here, Ma was frantic and nervous. She forgot things: her cell, the mail, the alarm system. She made soup stock, which was extra work. She made us clean up the house and clear out the garage. She emptied the fridge of ancient leftovers. If she'd had more time, she would have remodelled all the bathrooms.

"You should have told us before last night about art school," she says without expression. "You know your father argues with your uncles about everything: who bought the bigger house or the faster car, or whose kids got the higher grades or the better computer."

"No matter when I told him, he would have said no."

We talk without making eye contact. Ma knows I'm right. Passing the noisy food court, she asks. "Why don't you show him your photographs?"

"For sure he'll hate them."

"Let me see them."

"You'd hate them too."

"Would I?"

"My pictures, they show people, ordinary people, workers in kitchens, restaurants and stores. The photos, they are black and white. You won't like them."

"How about your portraits of Grandmother?"

"They won't change his mind."

"Those pictures of Grandmother, I liked them."

"Ba always wins," I mutter.

"If you really want to go to art school, then *I'll* pay your tuition."

"You don't have enough money." She's not serious. She can't be. We keep walking at the same pace. I'm distracted by the window displays, checking out what's new.

"I do," she insists.

"I don't want your money."

"But you'll take it from your father?"

"He's working in Taipei to make tuition money for me and Homer. If he stopped, he could get a job selling insurance here."

"Coming in?" Ma stops at the supermarket. She knows I hate grocery shopping.

"I'll wait here."

"I'm serious about paying your tuition."

●

My father lives one continent and one ocean away, yet runs my life as if he owns the world's most powerful remote control. He wants to be a parent, but what he really wants is success, to present a good face, for people to line up and shake his hand, to congratulate him on the success of his children.

Sure, I want my parents to be happy. I'm not ungrateful. I know immigration was tough. I know the big move was done for us kids. It cost money. Their marriage suffered. Ma was forced to learn English. Even now, she calls herself an immigrant—even though she has citizenship and pays taxes. Is she happy? She says, "If you're happy, then I'm happy."

Is Ba happy? Who knows? Who cares? He works long hours, lives alone and flies back and forth on thirty-hour flights like an astronaut. If he lived here with us, maybe I would go to university. If he slaved in Chinatown at mini-wage, had a boss shout at him all day long and had customers treat him like an insect, I'd want to do more for him. But he's a banker sitting in an office. A secretary answers his telephone. He doesn't need a thing from me. Sure, a doctor daughter would make him look noble. The last thing Ma should do is pay for my education. That would be a sure-fire path to Ba losing face, and this astronaut family has enough trouble already.

Crystal Yeh walks by. She stops to chat and show off her new boyfriend. He's really tall. He's already at university. When she asks about my plans for the fall, I shrug and say nothing is certain. She's the lucky one. She's got a summer job, and her parents are letting her do fashion design. Everyone says she's got talent: kids in her class were fighting to model pieces from her collection at the senior fashion show. If only my parents were like her parents.

•

At dinner, Ba asks, "How many more universities are you waiting to hear from?"

I take my time chewing and swallowing before I answer. "Two."

"Liu Rong-wen says his daughter is going to Harvard."

"Daughter's photographs are very good," Ma says, breaking her silence. "You should look at them."

Ba slams his hand onto the table. The dishes rattle. "I would rather see the money people will pay for them."

"She's still learning," Ma persists. "That's why there's art school."

Ba throws down his chopsticks and addresses me. "I gave you far too much freedom. You didn't want to study Chinese. I let you quit. You wanted to play basketball. I let you join the team. You wanted to learn to drive. I said yes. But university is one thing I won't compromise on. If I do, you'll regret it forever."

Forever. When they want to scare you, they say forever. So final. So far away.

•

K.S. phones me and asks me to visit Uncle Foon. He's not happy to see me. He doesn't even want me inside his house. He's cranky, but that's his nature. When I first met him, I had no idea his work had been featured in *Life* magazine sixty years ago. The faces of Mao and Chiang, the two sides of China's civil war, were strangers to me. Uncle Foon had asked me to make some copy prints because his negatives had been lost—remarkable photos of refugees, bombed-out cities, soldiers, bloated corpses and child beggars from China's long war.

Now I'm wheedling him. "You helped me in Chinatown," I say. "You still care for the community."

"Leave me alone," he grunted.

The tiny living room has a dusty, sagging sofa and an oversized TV showing a Chinese soap opera. Hundreds of video cassettes are piled on the floor, on tables, on shelves. Spindly plants that were once green sit on a wooden box by the window, framed by grimy curtains. The air is heavy with the old-people smell of white-flower oil.

I have to compete against the TV screen for his attention. "You helped me. Why can't you do K.S. a favour this one time?"

"I helped him. I let him show my photos!"

"People want to meet you. You're famous."

"They can see my photos."

"Photos are just paper and chemicals. You are flesh and blood."

"You are full of BS."

I don't understand why Uncle Foon ever bothered to help me. We're from different generations, different backgrounds and even different parts of town. He knows people in Chinatown, but he's always alone. I've never seen anyone greet him or even drink coffee with him.

I try again. "You know, if I took pictures one-quarter as good as you, I'd want my entire family to see them."

"You speak nonsense."

"Don't you want to inspire your grandchildren?"

"Don't have any."

I point to pictures on his wall, on the mantel. "Who are those people?"

"Nephews, nieces."

"Don't you care about them?"

"No."

He's as stubborn as my father, and now there's the same cold indifference between us.

"Leaving now?" he asks. "Good, take those cakes you brought. I don't want them."

I'm out of tricks. I get to my feet, and he stands up to show me the door. Then he says, "Wait."

When he comes back, he hands me something heavy but compact. It's an old-fashioned camera case, stiff and dried. Its contents are a pleasant surprise: a Leica M3, the camera responsible for the best pictures taken since the 1950s. It's an engineering masterpiece, a collector's item.

"This is a beauty," I say. "People still use it today."

I play with it and heft it in my hand. It's solidly built and perfectly balanced. I peer through the viewfinder, and, even in the dimly lit room, it focuses easily and clearly.

"This is worth a lot of money, did you know that?"

"It's a gift. Now go. Hurry."

I hand it back to him. "No."

He hides his arms behind his back. "Take it."

"No, I have a camera."

"If you don't take it, I will throw it in the garbage."

He's grinning happily. Has he gone crazy? I shake my head. "It's your camera; you do whatever you want."

"I want you to use it."

"I'm not going to art school. I won't be a photographer."

"Don't say that!"

"Don't tell me what to do!"

I throw the camera on the sofa and rush out. Grown-ups earn money; they buy expensive stuff; they acquire reputations; and then they want to dictate to young people what to do. Didn't they ever suffer at the hands of *their* fathers? Or is this just revenge?

•

When I get home, Homer is lounging in the family room, watching TV. His eyes don't leave the screen as he mutters, "You're going to art school. Happy?"

I don't know what he's talking about.

He flings a bundle of paper at me. It's the magazine from *World View*, one of several Chinese newspapers competing for readers in the GTA. Every week it publishes a glossy supplement containing longer stories, human-interest features, photo spreads and local content. There on the cover is my portrait of Uncle Foon, sitting on his sofa, holding up one of his photographs from sixty years ago. K.S. must have sent out my picture to publicize the exhibition.

The headline reads: *Treasure Trove Unearthed Nearby*.

"This won't change Ba's mind," I say.

"Grandmother overheard him telling Ma how proud he is of you now."

"He's always talking big."

"So that's it? You're giving up?"

I smiled. "Maybe not."

WE'RE DATING WHITE GUYS

Haven't opened this journal in a long time. Why bother? Nothing much happens in my pathetic life. School ended yesterday, thank God. And before I could even breathe, my first shift on full time started at eight this morning. Summer holidays? Hah! I'm getting up way too early. At least I've switched gears, right brain to left. Or is it left to right? Whatever. Being brain-dead works for me. Scan, cash, bag. Scan, cash, bag. *Meep-meep, clickety-click. Meep-meep, clickety-click* all day long. At least I'm out of the house; staying home all day with Ma would drive me totally nuts.

This summer I promise I'll lose weight. Then when I start university, I'll have a body to show off. The books say dropping twenty pounds in two months is doable. The books say if I keep a journal or join a chat room it will make it easier to lose weight. But it won't be easy. I work in enemy territory, and with my staff discount, chips and chocolates are way too cheap. Thank God for the cosmetic counter. One glance at the cream queens and I resolve to succeed. I should take up running, but Jeannie would die laughing.

She wants a summer job too. So I sent her to the Shoppers Drugmart website, but I hope she gets another store. Who wants their sister working with them?

June 29

What a shitty day. Toronto is sweating through its second heat wave already, and the heat and humidity are unbearable. I was hoping people would stay home with their air conditioning turned on full blast, but instead we had a steady stream of customers. A woman wanted to return knee supports. Too loose a fit, she said. But she had worn them until they were wrinkled and sweaty, totally gross. When I paged Stewart, he stuck his nose here and there, and then he approved the refund. With a big smile. The day before, he was picky as hell about everything. Forget the only-if-we-can-sell-it-again rule when it's a blonde. When she saw Stewart, her voice dropped from bitch-sharp to babe-smooth. Then she glared at me like, *Wasn't I right all along, you fat slob?*

She wouldn't have treated Tina Cowan like that.

Carol phoned to congratulate me on graduating. At first, she tried to do catch-up, asking about my job and would I tint my hair and was I still watching *Desperate Housewives*. I haven't seen her since February, when Kevin and his buddies performed at the Chinese New Year show.

Carol, as usual, is doing summer session at U of T. She still makes me look bad, same as she did when we were kids at Chinese folk dance, Chinese school and ballet. Or was it me being dumpy that made her look good? Carol wants to get together soon. I wish it were later so she could see the slimmer me.

I'm good today: fruit for breakfast, salad and canned fish for lunch and half a bowl of rice at dinner. No doughnuts, no chocolates.

JULY 3

Carol was late, so I was miffed. But what juicy news she had. She split with Kevin! She quit summer school! She wants to take a year off, totally quit sciences or even move far away. Whoa! Is this the dorky, preppy cousin I've known all my life? She's aimed for med school since grade three, planning to save lives, cure cancer and end suffering throughout the world.

Why? Why? Why? Was it Kevin?

"No," she said, "I just need time to myself to think things through."

Then she got all weepy. Whoa! Carol doesn't cry!

"This is really hurting him," she says. "He keeps saying let's figure this out. Let's fix this. But he doesn't know me at all. *Is there someone else?* No. *Are you bored with me?* No. *Did I do something to upset you?* No. *I thought you loved me.* I do. I do."

"Wait a minute," I said. "If you love him, why are you breaking up?"

She blew her nose. She looked awful (tee-hee!). "I don't know. We don't feel right anymore."

"Then you're not in love with him anymore," I said, as if I knew everything about love and boyfriends.

"But I am," she insisted. "And he knows it, and that's why he's not letting go."

I was totally confused, so we went shopping. She apologized for forgetting my birthday. I hadn't bought her anything either, but she had missed first, so it was her fault. Saleswomen in mile-high stilettos killed themselves trying to help Carol, thinking she would drop hundreds or thousands of dollars. She started on about Kevin again.

"Sooner or later we would have broken up," she said. "My folks don't really like him."

I had thought they were cool with him. "Why?"

She frowned. "You know why."

"Because he's white?"

Carol doesn't answer. She knows what I'll say.

"They're racist," I said. "If *his* parents didn't like you for being Chinese, we'd call them ugly names."

But she had drifted off into another aisle.

JULY 4

Today was my day off. I didn't know Ma had an appointment at Dr. Gullidge's. Jeannie and the cross-country runners went down to Lake Ontario where there's supposed to be a breeze. Jimmy went shopping for a new skateboard. So no one else could go with Ma. She wore her yellow suit. The magazines in the waiting room were as old as dinosaurs and sticky, so I washed my hands several times. Ma has visited Dr. G. by herself, so I don't know why she insists on someone coming to translate for her. Dr. G. told Ma to change her diet. But she won't, even though she nods at everything he says.

The fridge was full of greasy leftovers, so I had low-fat, low-sodium crackers and skim milk for lunch. Yuck! Ma doesn't eat a big lunch either. I skipped dinner. But now I'm going to get some crackers. It's bad eating so late, but if I don't, I can't sleep.

July 5

Bobby D'Amico asked me out!!! I'm singing in the rain!!!!! Wait. Kill all those !!!s! I'm cool, cool as a Popsicle, cool as a waterfall. I'm fabulously poised. I'm a cream queen. Bobby is the store's best merchandiser, always checking for stock when things run low. He's won the Customer Excellence Award a million times. During break, we were griping about the shifts when he said, "Wanna see a movie sometime? With me, that is?"

Next Thursday! Wait till I tell Carol. We're dating white guys!

Bobby is always joking and playing pranks, so everyone (including me, of course) likes him. He comes to work wearing black leather (he rides a motorcycle), and I'm not the only one watching the glow around his thighs. He changes into normal clothes in the washroom, but leaves his silver stud in his left ear. He has bright eyes, but part of his face is lumpy-bumpy with old pimples. But who cares about looks? I hope he feels the same about me. He must, otherwise why would he ask me out? Maybe he likes chubby girls. Maybe he's a freak.

We'll meet after work at the other end of the mall. We'll eat, hang out and catch a movie. I'll tell Dad I'm subbing for someone and the night manager will drive me home. Dad knows the routine.

It's no big deal. I'm not going crazy thinking about what to wear. I don't care if someone sees us at the mall. We're co-workers, that's all. Our shifts ended together, and we decided to catch a show. I'm even glad I haven't lost weight yet. That takes the pressure off. It's just a movie. Nothing more. Remember that before you completely make a fool of yourself.

Ma threw away her pills, seventy dollars' worth. She says they make her too tired to play a decent hand of mah-jongg. Why does she see the doctor if she dumps his advice? She likes being sick. It's her way of making us worry. Dad listens at the table, but words go in one ear and straight out the other. He gulps his food and heads to the garden to pick some flowers. Mom grumbles, "Useless. Better to buy the fresh-cut ones. All those insects, all that smelly earth tracked into the house. Who cleans it?" Dad doesn't say a word.

At dinner, I drank lots of soup and ate some veggies and some steamed fish. I managed to dump my rice because both Ma and Dad left the table early. They're mad at each other. So what else is new?

July 6

I'm glad Carol phoned tonight; it took my mind off the tub of ice cream Dad bought today.

Kevin went to her house and wouldn't go away until she let him in. He offered to quit kung fu. That must have been a big shock, because Kevin has gotten really good really fast. Well, it helped that he had been on the gymnastics squad. He asked her what he could do to make things work. She said, "Nothing."

Then she muttered how she hated him doing kung fu. I couldn't believe I'd heard right. This was the ex-president of the Multicultural Club talking?

It's supposed to be awesome for people to do different cultures: Kevin learning kung fu, Richard Soo playing bagpipes, Seanna leading the tabla group and everyone jamming on the *djembe* drums.

Now Kevin wants to quit school and go to China and study kung fu full time. He hangs around with Carson Hsiang and Micah Li, his new kung-fu buddies, all the time. Carol hates them. They were always too goofy, too loud for her.

"White parents let their kids do strange things," Carol said. "Even if it screws up their entire lives."

I didn't think she really wanted to break up, so I said, "Why don't you go with him? You could study Chinese there, like Adam Wu. His parents are sending him there for two years."

"Yeah, yeah. Companies around the world are doing business in China."

"Biggest market in the world."

Then Carol said something strange. "Kung fu should be about Asians looking good."

I didn't understand, but Carol waved her hand. "Forget it."

When I told her about Bobby, she asked, "Tell your family?"

"Are you kidding?"

JULY 7

Three pounds down already! Jeannie is eating leftovers for breakfast and I'm making a fruit platter when Ma comes in. Right away she says I'll never lose weight. I ignore her. Last night she was making noises about Hong Kong again. I don't know why she bothers going. All she does is bitch about the crowds, the lousy shopping and the long flight. If Dad didn't bring home airline passes, she wouldn't go.

I cheated at lunch and had some fries. Five, to be exact. But I didn't take any cake. It was Tanya's last day at the store, so we got her double-chocolate layer cake from Dufflets. Bobby went all the way down to Queen Street to pick it up. About half the cake got tossed out because everybody is dieting. I watched Bobby eat. He could stand to lose a few pounds, but who am I to talk? All the guys were pigging out, and he was too busy eating to talk to me. I ran to Gap to check out the sale. Stupid me, I forgot to dump my smock and looked like a total dork modelling my *Hi-how-can-JOYCE-help-you-today* name tag. I almost bought a new top for tomorrow night, but what's the point? I'm going to lose more weight before the summer is over.

Hu-lan came into the store today. Her last name is Xi or Xu or Xie, whatever. It's spelled funny. She's so out of it that she couldn't even look me in the eye. Lucky for her she wasn't buying tampons or deodorant! I doubt her English is good enough for university.

JULY 8

Bobby has awesome grey eyes. At the restaurant, I ordered salad and grilled chicken, while he had a New York steak with red wine. Whoa! I thought he'd be a brew boy. I told him how my face went all red when I drank. When we traded groan zone stories, he told one about a woman buying a load of stuff—toilet paper, tissues, hand cream, candies, whatever. When she opened her purse, a TV remote control fell out. The Customer Excellence cashier smiled and asked if she always carried it around.

The woman said, "My husband wouldn't come with me, so I'm getting even!"

Bobby wants to go back and get his Grade 12. Now he regrets dropping out. He was a skateboarder then, flipping and hanging loose all day. He has four siblings. His favourite bands are Coldplay, Our Lady Peace and Radiohead. He eats Chinese food and loves chicken with black-bean sauce. On TV, he watches *The Simpsons, Trailer Park Boys* and *Law and Order: CI.*

He asked if my family minded me seeing a white guy. I told him my cousin had dated one since high school. I didn't mention that Carol didn't tell her parents until a year later and besides Kevin was an honour student and was supposed to go east for university.

Bobby went to a Catholic high school but ended up dropping out. But he doesn't blame the school; he blames himself for being a jerk.

When I asked him about university, he said, "I'll be lucky if I can get my Grade 12."

Stupid me, I asked, "So, how long do you want to work in the store?"

Whoa, girl! He's five years older!

He said he wanted to see the world.

"Wow," I said. "Expensive." From stupid to stupider to stupidest, that's me. Would both my feet fit in my mouth? Good thing I didn't mention motorcycle gangs.

"Do you think I could teach English? I hear there are lots of jobs in Korea. People check out the place, and then they move on. They go to Taiwan. They teach there, and then they move on and go to Japan. That's so cool."

I think you need a TESL certificate but didn't say so. I mean, English is his first (and only) language, right? And people in Asia want Caucasian teachers. They hire them over Asians, even if the Asians were born here and speak nothing but perfect English.

He asked me where I came from, how often I travelled to Asia, how I learned to speak English so well and whether I watched Chinese movies. He told me I was the first Chinese girl he had dated. Was I supposed to feel good about that?

July 10

Saturday afternoon, Carol meets me after work, and we head to the food court. I grab a salad and a bottle of water from the pizza place. I make Carol change tables when I see Zhao Da-ren and his two sidekicks, Leon and

Ming, close by, scarfing down a bucket of KFC chicken. When I mention Bobby, she asks, "Is he cute?"

I must have avoided answering, because she asks again. So I say, "Yeah, kind of."

She's so fixated on looks. Today, she says her future boyfriend has to be her equal and have separate interests. That way, she says, she'll know if they're soulmates, connected at some deeper level. Sounds like she still wants to be with Kevin. Sex was great, she says. But she complains that he changed. First he got hooked on kung fu. Now he wants to go to China.

"What next?" asks Carol. "A career in action movies?"

Carol says long-term goals are important. She says she wants him to be happy, and since he's happiest doing kung fu now, she wouldn't care if he quit university. Kevin said he would quit martial arts for her, but she doesn't want him to. She'd rather break up. Go figure.

Carol notices that I get quiet, so we talk about Bobby. Friends of his in a band are playing at the Kensington Market Festival on Saturday, so I'm going. Carol says, "You don't know anything about music!"

I tell her I'll check things out on the net.

She doesn't think much of me and Bobby. So what if we have different backgrounds? Look at her: she and Kevin are turning out to be way more different than expected. Now she's looping around in circles. In high school, Carol was one of the few Chinese who hung with the white kids. I thought it was because she took drama and band and joined the volleyball team. I used to get so jealous when she went on out-of-town trips for tournaments. She moved like a ballerina, light and delicate. Year after year, she had the same look: white pants with white top, black pants with black top, always matching tops and bottoms. She didn't want to stand out.

July 11

Surprise! Jeannie wants to go to China! There's a program in August for high school students to learn Mandarin in Beijing. I can't imagine her doing this at all, but Dad of course thinks it's great. He warns her against changing her mind. Last year, she enrolled for guitar lessons and then quit. "Once you're in China," he says, "you can't leave until the date on your ticket. If you want to return earlier, you'll have to buy a one-way ticket. Very expensive."

Ma is a wet blanket. Nag, nag, nag. Blah, blah, blah. "Didn't I tell you to study Mandarin when you were little? It would have been easier, but you wouldn't listen.

Now it's going to be hard. Do you know how hot and dusty Beijing is? You're sure to complain. What about your allergies? What if you don't have air conditioning? If you're all students from overseas, you'll speak English all day long. You won't learn a thing."

Ma hates China. If the communists hadn't taken back Hong Kong, we never would have immigrated. Ma would still have her job. She always reminds us how she sacrificed everything so that we could move when Jeannie and I were young enough to learn English quickly. We still speak Cantonese with my parents. Not Carol. Her parents speak to her in Cantonese, and she answers only in English, just like Jimmy.

Jeannie in Beijing? I guess other kids go to camp, and Jeannie does need to get out of the house. So why shouldn't she go? Dad'll write her a blank cheque and seal it with a kiss. For him it's natural, it's totally logical. Chinese kids should speak, read and write Chinese. It's the way of the universe. Even if it doesn't really fit their lives.

Ma tries to sabotage my diet. Tonight, she asked me why I wasn't eating the shrimp-stuffed tofu, my all-time favourite. I told her, "It's fried."

"Oh," she said. "I forgot."

Yeah, as if.

July 13

Bobby caught a shoplifter. When I got to the store at four p.m., things were normal out front. But in the back, everyone was at the holding room door, trying to peek through the glass. Two cops arrived and told us to clear the way. I got my smock, and on my way out, the cops dragged out this thug-looking guy wearing an oversized hoodie, baggy pants and a jewellery rack in his ear. His hands were cuffed behind him. As I went by, he muttered, "Fucking Chink bitch."

I went cold all over. I hadn't been there when he got nabbed. Why should he snarl at me? What if he wanted revenge and came back and waited for me? He swore at the cops, using the N-word because one officer was black. The cop sighed and shook his head. "Move along, kid," is all he said.

At the back door, Bobby called out, "Thanks, Officer. Sorry for what he called you."

"No need to apologize," came the answer. "You didn't do anything."

Stewart said Bobby saw the guy tuck condoms and antiperspirant into his shirt. Then the guy casually strode to the magazine rack, checked out a few titles and paid for two chocolate bars. As soon as he stepped out the front door, Bobby grabbed him. He and Stewart marched him into the back and called the cops.

I was so shaken that I ate a chocolate bar at break.

JULY 14

Carol is so self-centred. She has no idea that when I work till midnight, I can't fall asleep until one or two a.m. Even Mom lets me sleep in.

Carol phones at ten this morning and gives me a hard time for being in bed. Kevin has been phoning her. I tell her to call the police and say he's stalking her. Then I hung up.

So then she called me at work to say that when Kevin called, they talked for two hours. He still won't accept that they're finished. Yet she won't see him. He wants to get back together with her, which I'm sure makes her feel marvellous.

I think she's jerking Kevin around. Right now she wants him gone from her life. But he won't go, because she hasn't given him a good enough reason. I don't get it. They look good together. He loves Chinese culture. He can use chopsticks. He's more serious about China than Jeannie.

Carol says her mom wants her to get a job, now that she's not doing summer school. I don't know how she can stay home all day and not go completely crazy. I wind up eating crackers for lunch again. Yuck!

JULY 18

Bobby's friends are spaced out and always drunk, but nice and lots of fun. Bones is the skinniest guy I've ever met, like a broomstick, with wisps of bleached-out hair. Already, he's losing hair, so he wears a baseball cap all the time. He's quiet. Kyle is like Bobby, always telling jokes and stories. He's with Shawna, who has a full-colour tiger tattoo covering her entire forearm. Her friend Cherry has hair tinted blue to match her nail polish. I can't believe they're all from the separate school system.

By the time Bobby and I met up with them, they were all pretty happy, having just left the beer garden. Kensington is funky because its ethnic stores and recycled clothes shops attract different crowds: preppy students, Goths, trendy condo owners. When the band came on, our crowd whistled and yelled like cowboys. The band played right through their racket and never stopped. They weren't too psycho. They wore black tee-shirts and black jeans. The band is called *Bad As*. They were good. Or, as they prefer, they were ba-ad. Mostly they played heavy-duty rock and roll and danced around the stage. At one point, Kyle leaned over and said, "You know how they say Chinese people can't drink? Bullshit! One night, I watched this Chinese guy chug twenty bottles of brew, one after another, no stopping, no food in between. And then he went on stage and sang *Moon River*!"

At one point, the guys went for more beer, leaving me with the girls. Cherry said, "Bobby likes college girls. He thinks we're too stupid for him."

"I'm pretty stupid too," I said. "A customer once asked me for the time, and I told him to go look in the magazine rack."

She laughed, so she wasn't dumb at all. I didn't mind her thinking that I was older.

They're a close bunch. They hang onto each other like a dance formation, arms around each other's shoulders. They must go back a long ways. The girls kiss everyone, guys and girls alike. Shawna asked if junkies ever get jobs working at the pharmacy counter. I said everything was locked up and the other staff aren't allowed in there.

Cherry asked, "Is it true that Chinese people like to eat dogs?"

I told her of course not.

She said, "I didn't think so. It's something I heard when I was little."

"What about snakes?" asked Shawna.

I told her that Chinese believed snakes were so powerful that eating their flesh would warm people in the wintertime.

Bobby and I left when he said he was starved. We went to Chinatown for dried fried beef noodles. He ate it with chili sauce. I didn't want to seem fussy about the food, so I ate some too. Then he dropped me off at the drugstore just before midnight, and I phoned Dad to come get me.

JULY 20

Jeannie got offered a job at the Danforth and Main store, and she might take it because she wants to buy new skis. She hasn't told Dad yet. He thinks she's getting in touch with her roots and heritage. Hah!

Wayne Lin and Andy Liang came in today, looking totally fried and sunburned. They think they're such hot jocks. No doubt they came from the beach. When they saw me, they went to the other cashier. Jerks. Taiwanese kids think they're so cool speaking Mandarin. I should switch stores and get out of this neighbourhood. Too many people know me here. Still, I was feeling cheerful, so I called out to them and waved goodbye when they were at the exit. They ran off like guilty shoplifters. Jerks!

Mom still wants to go to Hong Kong. She and Fourth Aunty might do Thailand after her kids are out of school for the summer. I told Mom she should go, even though I can't see Mom doing the beach scene in Phuket. She's way too squeamish, way too fussy. She'd get sick there, and we'd have to air-ambulance her home. But to have her out of town this summer would be great!

The diet is going really well. Believe it or not, I'm actually getting used to skim milk. The trick is to drink it while it's cold. Once it warms up, it's deadly.

July 22

Carol calls me at the store and asks what time I finish. She wants to grab a bite. I was hoping to hang out with Bobby, but his shift ends later, so we go to the food court. She orders pizza, but I go to the salad bar. Then she lays this on me. She's going to a movie with Carson, and wants me to come along with Micah.

I'm dumbfounded. "You hate Carson," I remind her. She blamed him for getting Kevin into kung fu.

She shrugged. "He's working out at the university this summer."

"You always say he needs another shower."

"Well, he sweats way too much. Tell him which deodorant sells the most."

"No way. And why would I go out with Micah? I'm seeing Bobby."

"You're not serious about him, are you?"

"We're going to the Tragically Hip concert."

"Micah could take you."

"Micah's a jerk."

Carol finishes her slice of pizza and wipes her fingers clean. She glares at my salad. "You shouldn't be dieting to make him happy."

"I started before he ever asked me out!"

"Whatever." Carol takes a long sip of her Coke. She looks up with a sly smile. "Carson says Micah really likes you."

"Yeah, right."

"He's shy."

"He's a loser."

"His profs want him to apply for grad school already."

"Good for him."

"Listen to me, Joyce. You and Bobby aren't going to work out. Once you go back to school, he'll dump you."

Carol has never shown any interest in helping me with guys, so I don't know what she's doing. "What does Kevin think about Carson asking you out? Does he know?"

"Who cares? He's a jerk."

"You said you still love him."

"He loves kung fu more."

For half a second everything is crystal clear. The last piece of the puzzle falls into place. All the bits and pieces of colour and corners become one image. "I know why you're breaking up with Kevin," I said. "Because he's becoming more Asian than you."

She frowns at me.

My words pour out: "Kevin has Chinese friends, he likes Chinese food and now he wants to study in China. He's going all out for something he wants, even if it looks strange. But you, you're the opposite. All your life, you've tried to be invisible. Your room is all white. Your clothes are plain. You're nice to everyone. You don't get into trouble. Kevin was perfect until he became the one thing that didn't fit your world. A high-profile Asian."

"He's not Asian, he's a white guy," said Carol. "What's this got to do with Bobby?"

"Nothing," I say.

DEATH SEEMS TO LINGER

I WAS FOUR YEARS OLD WHEN MY PARENTS DIED. HARD-AS-LEATHER FIRST AUNTY SAID, "YOUR PARENTS AREN'T COMING BACK. YOU'LL LIVE WITH US. MELISSA AND JENNY WILL BE YOUR OLDER SISTERS. WILL YOU LIKE THAT?"

I nodded.

"You'll have your own room. Will you like that?"

Yes.

"You can call me 'Ma.' Will you like that?"

I shook my head. No.

Later, my grade-four best friend asked, "Why is your mother your aunty?"

After that, I called First Aunty and Uncle, Ma and Ba.

The deaths of my parents seem to linger.

I avoid movies and TV shows about the "other side." At horror films, my pals boo and hiss at the special effects, but I'm down on the floor. Long ago Melissa trapped me at the TV where ghosts were haunting a house. She pinned my arms so I couldn't cover my ears. She held me tight so

I couldn't run. I squeezed my eyes shut, but the people on screen screamed, and so did I. Melissa hissed, "You act just like your mother did, afraid of everything!"

●

My cousins are getting a good giggle. The family is dining at the Ruby Palace, and then Trevor and Keith are going to see *Undead Sea*. I've seen the trailers. Not for me!

"You're abnormal, Simon," Keith says. "Man, you've got to grow up."

"You're weird," says Trevor. "It's all make-believe. Movies aren't real."

"You're an embarrassment, man. We can't take you anywhere." Keith just checked his text messages, and three girls are meeting them at the theatre.

When the appetizers arrive, chopsticks fly into action. Ma hands me an envelope.

"Your Ah-Poh sent this," she says. That's birth-Mum's mother. "Do a count."

It's fat with large-denomination bills.

Arooooh! My cousins howl like wolves, ready to devour. Down, boys, down.

"Now, did everyone see?" Ma looks around the table. "You be witnesses. I don't want *her* saying I stole the money."

The way Ma spits out "her," you'd think Ah-Poh was doing time for murder or worse.

"She wants Simon to return to Hong Kong." Ma is as brittle as a plastic fork. "She says her health is bad. She says he should visit before university starts. Otherwise, she claims, he'll be too busy to ever go."

"She knows he graduated?" asks Second Aunty.

"That woman, she's a rat-chasing rice peddler."

There's more to come. From Ma, that is. It's strange that she's raising this touchy topic at dinner.

"Didn't she already pass away?" asks Grandmother.

"No, but she's crazy-crazy," advises Second Aunty. "From long ago to now."

"Simon's mother was like that too."

Ma tells birth-Mum's story again, to remind me of my good luck. "They say she was paralyzed with fear. She was right behind your father when the truck hit. She cradled him like a baby. She wailed, sobbing like a professional mourner. The blood soaked her dress, her hands, her legs. The ambulance men drove her to the hospital, thinking she was hurt too. Stupid girl, she left you behind. You know how busy Wanchai Road is. So easy for someone to kidnap you."

I ask, "You were there?"

"It was the other side's banquet. They didn't invite us."

"So how do you know about her crying and me on the sidewalk?"

A waiter removes the empty platter, and another one steps up to ladle the soup.

Third Aunty asks, "Ah-Fong didn't have to kill herself, did she? She could have lived with any one of us."

Third Uncle knew her well. "She was too thick-necked." He speaks between slurps of soup. "She wanted to live alone, but couldn't find a job. She registered for school, but didn't attend. She said she wouldn't re-marry, but she kept smiling at men."

Grandmother rests her spoon. "I told her to come live with me. Many times. I don't know what she was afraid of."

Second Uncle says, "She married too early. Just eighteen, what could she know? She never worked. All she cared about was new clothes. We never asked her to babysit our two children."

Second Aunty exclaims, "She's dead, and now you know everything? She was ten times smarter than you!"

Second Uncle, a college professor, takes no offence.

"Simon, will you go?" Ba is an engineer, a man of few words. He speaks when people are bogged down and can't make a decision. "You decide for yourself." He pauses. "It's a good opportunity, you know that?" He pauses again. It drives me bonkers. "After your Ah-Poh dies, no one will invite you to stay."

"If I don't go, do I have to return the money?"

"The money was sent for plane fare. If you don't go, you should tell her yourself."

"If he doesn't want to go, then he doesn't have to go!" Ma snaps.

"Then the money should be sent back," Ba says sharply.

Silence follows. Third Aunty refills the boys' bowls. We cousins are still viewed as youngsters, so we are expected to eat a lot. The grown-ups merely taste the dishes so that they can critique them later.

I'm not inclined to go. In Toronto, we have everything Hong Kong has: food, CDs, electronics, magazines and clothes. Kids who get dragged back to Asia don't like it at all. You can't drive there with a Level One licence. Trapped with family, you're stuck at tons of boring visits while the adults yak. Unless you're FOB, you have no friends there.

●

That night, no matter how loud my boom box blasts Coldplay, the words "crazy-crazy" stay in my head. I stare at the wad of bills. I've never seen so much money. I can hold it. It's mine to spend. I could do something new: travel by myself. Come the fall, other kids will be living in dorms and partying. Me, I'll be at home. Here's a chance for a solo trip abroad. I'd be crazy to give up the money.

Being labelled "crazy" is serious. It's permanent damage to your reputation. What's crazy is that birth-Mum killed herself when she had pulled off the ultimate deed for the family. She had produced a male heir: a son to carry on the name. That's why Aunty adopted me: Uncle wanted a boy with his surname. Birth-Mum would have enjoyed high status; our family would have treated her like royalty. Didn't she love me?

If birth-Mum and her mother are crazy-crazy, where does that leave me? Am I doomed to follow? Last winter I rented *The Sixth Sense* and forced myself to watch it with Melissa. I bet her twenty dollars I could last until the end. I did, but I shook like a baby. Next day I watched four Disney movies back-to-back.

This is supposed to be my best summer ever. For once, I'm not dragging my ass through summer school. To everyone's surprise, I landed a job with Parks and Rec, herding kids through day camps. I'm at the Gordon Community Centre, right on the Sheppard subway line, so it'll be easy taking the kids out on field trips. Guess who else is working there? Crystal Yeh, whom I almost asked to grad. That is, until Dandy-Andy stepped all over me. My ears burn and my tongue goes numb whenever she opens her locker, three down from mine. She's in fashion design and is going to the Pratt in New York in September.

I see my skinny face in the mirror. Guys like Eric Wu and Lincoln Wen have been having sex for ages. I'm still (dare I say it?) a virgin. Jeffrey landed a summer job at Eddie Bauer, and I'm taking seven-year-olds into wading pools. What a joke! In the fall, he's going to Africa on an exchange program to do development work. He's getting shots for malaria, hepatitis, yellow fever, typhoid fever. The other night, Ba was talking about someone's son from Hong Kong. A seventeen-year-old married a girl to help her family immigrate. Now the kid is a father. Seventeen! Is he even shaving yet?

I'll go for two weeks. I'll be back in August to see Crystal and work at camp. I can say, "Yeah, just got back from Hong Kong." She's from Taiwan, so I can say, "Ever been to Hong Kong?"

•

It's a long flight. Joyce Koo's mother is on board, on the other side of the plane. I met her at grad, and even then she looked sick: pale, thin and shaky. She looks worse now. The movies are *Curse of the Dead* and *Demon Dog.* I try to watch them, but I get the worst headache known to man, and I'm sick until I deplane. The fresh air revives me, as does my first take of the locals. All the customs and passport officers look to be about my age, even younger, only they wear uniforms and act very serious. They're like Boy Scouts with clout.

Will my relatives recognize me? Long ago we received Christmas cards and badly focussed photos. The faces were the size of ladybugs.

In the reception hall, I look for a familiar face. Then someone shrieks, "Siu-jeung, is that you? Siu-jeung, is that you?"

It's no exaggeration to say shriek. Passengers grab their children protectively. A woman sprints toward me. She's wearing white Nikes. She seizes my hands. She bursts into tears. "He came back. He came back."

Her voice is like gravel, husky like a long-time smoker's. "He really came back," she chants happily, dancing from one foot to the other. "My grandson really came back."

Ah-Poh's face is darkly tanned and plump, with shiny cheeks. Her hands are warm and slightly damp. I smell White Flower Oil. She bounces up and down. She doesn't look sick. I smell a scam. Her white hair hangs straight to her shoulders, held back with bobby pins. Her purple-and-black polyester suit is sneered at by everyone in our generation. How did my princess birth mother marry the son of this peasant?

"Are you Simon?" A girl stands next to her. She looks my age and has gold and maroon highlights in her hair. "I'm Monica, your elder cousin."

She's pretty, with dimples and a tiny mouth. Nice body too. She dabs at Ah-Poh's eyes with tissue as if Granny is a toddler. "Didn't I say, right away you'd find him?"

"He looks just like his father!" My grandmother grabs me. "Have a girlfriend?"

"No."

"And before?"

"No."

"Why?"

What do I say? That I turn into wood around girls? That everyone thinks I'm a geek? That if you want to get into a good university, there's no time for fooling around?

Ah-Poh's eyes drill into me. "Are you needing Ah-Poh to help you find a girl?"

"No!"

Monica laughs to herself.

"Are we getting a cab?" I demand.

Ah-Poh asks, "How long will you stay?"

"Two weeks."

"So short!"

"Very difficult to find a ticket." I don't mention Ma's marathon hunt to get the cheapest ticket ever issued on this planet. "This is the busy season for travel."

"Stay longer!"

"Ticket can't be changed."

My grandmother snorts. "Ah-Poh will buy another ticket for you."

I shake my head. "I have to go back. I have a summer job."

"What? Are you earning lots of money?"

I shrug. She declares, "Ah-Poh will give money to you."

"No." I try to sound assertive. "I can't stay longer."

She looks down, mumbling to herself. When she looks up, tears are streaming from her eyes. She lets loose a wail so piercing that I wince. She stamps her foot. "You came from so far, why not stay longer?"

I try to hush her, but she gets even louder.

"Some ten years, I haven't seen my bone and flesh," she screams at passersby. "Now he won't stay longer! Is there any justice in this world? Some ten years, I haven't seen my grandson, and he wants to leave already!"

I want to vanish! This woman *is* crazy! Puzzled strangers skirt by us. Ah-Poh's eyes are red and puffy. Don't old folks go blind from over-crying?

Monica is striding away. "Talk later!" she calls.

Eventually Ah-Poh follows us, pouting like a toddler.

I think it was a mistake coming here. It's confirmed when the climate slams into me. We take the train into town and then jump into a taxi. Then we exit, hurry into an apartment block and ride the elevator. Two hops and I'm drenched in sweat. The heat and humidity are a steam bath. Ah-Poh, on the other hand, is as dry as powder. When the apartment door opens, I see a crowd. I want to do an about-face and run home.

Too many *Yee-mahs* and *Yee-jeungs* are present, plus plenty of non-relatives, enough for three tables of mah-jongg and a bleacher of loud onlookers. They nod curtly at me. I've seen more spirit at school assemblies. Children sit at a large-screen TV watching a cop movie. Assault rifles pound over the clatter of mah-jongg tiles. A cellphone rings and adds to the racket.

Monica takes me around the apartment. I get Ah-Poh's room. There's one bathroom for six people.

I call home on my cell to let Ma know I arrived safely. She got me a long-distance plan at the lowest rate. "Don't use their phone," she ordered. "Don't get into debt to them."

I never suspected birth-Mum's family was so badly off. The mah-jongg tables, fold-up chairs and TV are the only furniture in the room. No sofa, no La-Z-Boy, no coffee tables, no lamps. The children sit on the floor between the gaming tables. At least there's air conditioning. It rumbles noisily, adding another layer to the din. The firm mattress feels like iron.

There's a faint knock at my door. Ah-Poh comes in. Has she calmed down?

"Such an inadequate welcome," she says quietly. "You come from so far away, and then stay in such shabby conditions. It really is an inadequate welcome."

She presses a bundle into my hand. It's money, Hong Kong dollars. I push it back.

Her voice breaks. "Ah-Poh has nothing much to give you. Ah-Poh knows you young people live in a different world. No matter what I buy, you won't like it."

"Don't buy me anything," I say. "I came to see you. I thought you were sick."

"Sick? Me?" She straightens up, indignant. "I haven't been sick for tens of years," she says. "Who said I was sick?"

"My mother."

"Her?" She snorts. "What else does she say about me?"

I don't go near that one.

"Your mother was a good girl. When Ah-Fong was little, she went to the church door for us. Sometimes she brought back rice and flour, sometimes milk powder and noodles. Sometimes soap. Every week it was different, whatever had been donated."

Let me guess. She also knelt on the street, shining men's shoes.

"Only adults could receive the charity, but I was busy. Fong went with her little brother. The minister was good-hearted and gave her food. One time, some boys pushed her over and stole the food. Ah-Fong went back to church to ask for more, but nothing was left. She was so afraid that she hid on the roof. We spent the night on the streets calling her name. We thought she had been kidnapped. Wasn't she good?"

Yeah, what an angel.

"When you were born, the smile on her face lasted for months. She loved you very much."

So why'd she kill herself?

Her head jerks up.

Oh God! Did I say that aloud?

She asks, "How long will you stay?"

"Two weeks."

"So little time? Stay longer!"

Has she forgotten already? Patiently, I remind her about the job.

"You'll have time to work in the future. Do you know, every night for ten years and more Ah-Poh has thought about you? I call out your name every night. I can die in peace now that I've seen you."

The curtains are drawn, and the light is dim. There's a plastic wall unit to one side, with shelves of biscuit tins, photo albums, cellophane-wrapped sweaters, figurines and stuffed animals, including one of Garfield the Cat (go figure). A clothes rack occupies one end of the room, because there is no closet, and it's jammed to capacity. Over the bed hang calendars, photographs, calligraphy calling for long life and prosperity and landscapes made from feathers and seashells.

"Have a girlfriend?"

Not this again! I grit my teeth as we replay this conversation.

"You like Chinese girls or white girls?"

"Both!"

"If you marry a Chinese girl, your grandfather and father in heaven will be happier."

•

In the following days, we repeat this conversation. I lose count of how many times. There are three topics: birth-Mum was a good girl; I should stay longer; and I need a girlfriend. Each time, Ah-Poh speaks with enthusiasm, as if the thought has just struck her, as if she'll run out and take action right away. She listens attentively, as though absorbing my answers into the deepest marrow of her bones. Fifteen minutes later she asks the same questions.

When I tell her my plans, she shakes her head. "Not the ocean. Not the beach."

It doesn't matter that I can swim, that I've had lifeguard training, that the boats provide life-jackets, that the Hong Kong tourism authority says it's all safe.

"Our surname, do you know what it means?" Ah-Poh asks.

"Forest."

"And where do forests grow?"

"On land."

"Land people ought not go on water."

"But I have a different surname."

Her word is final.

One night I stay up really late so I can get back into our gang's chat room. I tell them about my list: go cruising to see white dolphins, get a funky Chinese tattoo (small one), go shark-spotting at Sai Kung, check out the view from the windowed urinals atop the Peninsula Hotel. They're all groaning about the latest heat wave in Toronto, how nobody wants to go outside, how the city has ordered people not to water their lawns or wash their cars. I tell them it's almost 40 degrees here.

Ah-Poh and Monica take me to the cemetery. It's sunny, not a cloud in the sky. I've always found graveyards creepy, even in the daytime. To my surprise, birth-Mum and her father are buried in a Catholic cemetery, across from the racetrack, flanked by heavy traffic. The site is mostly concrete walls and cement steps. At tightly spaced plots, marble markers hold small portraits of the deceased.

In a loud voice, Ah-Poh calls to her loved ones: "Ah-Lung, Ah-Fong, I've brought Siu-jeung to see you. Look, look how he's tall and healthy. I know you've waited a long time. Now I hope you're satisfied. Please, rest contented. Please, protect us all."

I'm thinking, this is a Catholic cemetery; you can't talk like that! People are staring at us! If a guard hadn't been watching, no doubt Ah-Poh would have smuggled in incense, candles and food offerings.

Tears stream down her face. "This family of ours," she laments to a 50-storey tower, "has waited fifteen years for the three generations to reunite. It shouldn't be so. Really, it shouldn't be so. We should be together, helping one another, caring for one another."

One of her fists pounds the marker. Some graves are above the ground in concrete crypts; others have crosses and cherubs standing at surface level.

Ah-Poh wails on. "Siu-jeung moved to North America. He's far away. That's why it's taken him so long to return.

Everyone in Hong Kong has gone abroad, all the lucky ones. We are thankful Siu-jeung had the chance to return. Our family tried to emigrate, but no one could score enough points. In the fall, Siu-jeung starts university, so please ensure he does well at school."

When we're ready to leave, Ah-Poh lifts her arms, spreads them and trots around the two graves like a child playing airplane. Round and round she goes, humming like an engine. One arm goes up as the other one goes down. Won't she get dizzy and fall? Ah, she's had practice. Isn't this disrespectful? People are watching. My cellphone rings, but there's only a dial tone. I nudge my cousin. "What's she doing?"

"My father says it's like a mother bird looking after her nest."

"She's crazy!"

●

Monica keeps me sane. She's between jobs, so we see the Hong Kong Museum, tour the Peak and visit glitzy shopping malls. I get lost, but our cellphones save the day. She's only a year older but very confident, very poised. She asks if I want to visit Shenzhen, China's shopping paradise. Ma told me not to, because she's convinced that China is hiding the truth about avian flu.

Monica has friends who have emigrated, so she knows how we live abroad. Hong Kong is familiar to me, given the thousands of movies and TV shows I've seen, so I can ask decent questions. I tell her that Ba is a bit distant, but he's the same with my sisters. Melissa and Jenny always treated me like a real brother, jealous I had my own room and tormenting me until they discovered real boys.

Monica says Ah-Poh is old, so she's not all there. She watches TV but doesn't recall names or plots. She dines out with the family but doesn't recall new restaurants. She insists on washing her clothes by hand. Monica's parents and sister are rarely home, and when they are, they snap at Ah-Poh.

"I told you I don't want breakfast," shouts the sister.

"I'll wash the dishes," the mother insists. "You try to save hot water and the dishes aren't clean."

"Put away your shoes," orders the father. "Don't leave them at the front door so everyone trips over them."

When I phone Ma again, she asks, "Are you having fun?"

I tell her, "Of course; I'm in Hong Kong."

"What's the best thing so far?"

"Sleeping in every morning."

Truth is, the best thing so far is Monica and her boyfriend, Danny. Those two are so in love that it makes me ache. Sure, they hold hands, and I've seen couples in school do the same and cuddle in the hallways. But with Monica and Danny, it's how they sit close while sitting in a booth; it's how they feed each other choice bits of food without asking. Danny is a technician with Canon, so he's on the road a lot of the time.

"If you want to hook a girl," Danny says, "you must have big-male flavour."

"You think you've got it?" Monica asks, teasing.

"It's how you walk; it's how you look at the girl; it's how you take care of her."

"Give me an example."

"You should never be late," he declares. "And if you are, call her on her cellphone."

"That's not big-male flavour," says Monica. "That's just good manners."

Danny tries again. "When you arrive somewhere and park, and there's no attendant, you should say, 'Wait, let me come around and open the door.'"

"You don't do that!" Monica retorts.

"I do it all the time. You just don't notice."

We all laugh.

Monica and Danny know where kids gather to ride skateboards or do hip hop. Faye Wong does a concert one night, and we join thousands of fans at the stadium. In the apartment, the TV is always on, so it feels just like home.

Ah-Poh insists on shopping, forcing me to choose clothes that she can buy for me. I dread going with her: what if she starts quacking like a duck or ripping off her own clothes? As we trek from shop to shop, Ah-Poh again asks about girlfriends and staying longer. She gets short of breath, and we sit down. I panic and think that if she sickens, then I'll have no choice but to stay longer. But she gets back on her feet.

It's the same conversation when we go pay respects to birth-Dad. His ashes are out in the New Territories. The bus winds through green hills, but the haze never lifts. As soon as we arrive, Ah-Poh stops talking. I've never seen her so quiet. It's a *National Geographic* kind of temple, with flaring roofs, gigantic bronze urns and huge doors studded with brass plugs the size of toilet seats. Monks stroll through the steady thrum of Buddhist chants. Inside, it's the safety-deposit-box room of the bank, with rows and rows of small drawers. Markers display photographs, and right away I recognize birth-Dad.

Ah-Poh watches me do the three formal bows. Then she rushes off.

Monica says Ah-Poh didn't like birth-Dad much. "She said Ah-Fong shouldn't have married him. He didn't have a good job. He promised her things but never had money. He used to bully his mother for money."

•

I avoid Ah-Poh for the last few days, afraid she'll get frantic about my leaving. I do a last-minute sprint of shopping, scooping up DVDs and CDs at bargain prices. Danny gets me a hefty discount on a digital camera loaded with features. I give Ah-Poh my graduation portrait. She vows to keep it by her bed and look at it first thing when she wakens.

On departure day, Monica and Ah-Poh come to see me off. The train ride to the airport is quiet, as though we're withdrawing from one another or afraid of crying. I check my bags, and then we stop at the security gate. I hug Monica but can't quite do it with Ah-Poh.

She holds my hands and says, "Thank you for coming all this way to visit this old granny. You've made me very happy."

"I'm happy too," I tell her.

"Then why don't you stay longer?"

I can't believe she's still going on about this.

She grabs my arm. "Your family thinks your birth mother was crazy. Not so. She knew our family would have cared for her, would have cared for you. But she also knew our family couldn't offer much. You saw how we live. Your mother wanted a better life for you. So she killed herself. She knew your father's people would take you abroad. She had no other way to help you. It was her only way to show how much she really loved you."

Suddenly my cellphone rings. When I answer, there's only a dial tone. I freeze, and listen to the buzz. It feels like someone here wants to talk to me.

The next thing I know, tears are streaming from my eyes. It's the only time I've cried since coming here. I turn and head for the gate.

READING THIS NOVEL MADE ME HAVE SEX

"WHY DID MARGARET ATWOOD CHOOSE TO SET THIS STORY IN AMERICA?" MS. SANDHU ASKS THE CLASS. NOT A SINGLE STUDENT RESPONDS. SHE NEEDS A VOLUNTEER. SO SHE LOOKS AROUND, AND HER GAZE LANDS ON ME. "WHAT ABOUT YOU, JULIE SUNG?"

I stare into my book. Words blur. I feel Eric Wu looking at me.

"Don't be shy," Ms. Sandhu says, smiling. "Say whatever pops into your mind. Take a chance. Trust yourself."

I am not shy. I *have* read the novel, and I understand her question perfectly. But I don't have an answer—just a question. Am I pregnant? I will know by lunchtime.

We're studying *The Handmaid's Tale*. It's all about sex, and I had to use my Chinese/English dictionary a lot to make sure I understood every word. The story is set in the future, when many women can't have babies. So America's rulers force healthy young women to sleep with married men who are not their husbands in order to provide them with a child. I read it so fast that I surprised myself. I know what it's like to have every moment of your life controlled by someone else.

I think the novel is set in America because it's the most powerful nation in the world, because Americans make the best movies and TV shows and because Americans are sexually liberated.

But these may not be the answers Ms. Sandhu wants to hear. *The Handmaid's Tale* has been published in Chinese, and Shelley has a copy that she does not dare bring to school. Even if I had read the Chinese version, I still wouldn't be sure what answer Ms. Sandhu wants.

"Well, Julie?" Ms. Sandhu is still looking at me. "Was America a good place to set this novel?"

The teachers want immigrant students to speak out and voice their opinions. They say that students must have these skills to succeed at university. In China, if you did not have the right answer, you kept quiet. In Canada, Ms. Sandhu says that there is no single correct response and that every comment has some value. But I think there must be a proper reply to her question, and that is what she wants.

Ms. Sandhu comes closer. She is a good teacher. She maintains order in the classroom, and the troublemaker boys fear her. "What about China, Julie?" she asks.

"China?"

"Do you think this story could happen in China?"

"Oh, it is already happening. The government rule is that each family can only have one child."

"Very good!" She marches to the front. For some strange reason, teachers here believe they will succeed in building a class discussion if they start with a line that comes from a student. "Do people here know about China's one-child policy?"

•

After English class, Shelley and I head for calculus, but not Eric. He failed functions last year and again in summer school. He runs after us.

"Julie, you have to help me."

Shelley and I trade smiles that he can't see. We speak Putonghua, even though we're not supposed to.

"Have you read the novel, Eric?" I ask.

"Most of it."

That means he hasn't.

"You want to borrow my Chinese version?" Shelley asks.

"I haven't got any time to read it."

He doesn't want to talk to Shelley. He wants to talk to me.

"Can I call you tonight?" Eric asks.

"OK, but I can't talk long."

He grins. As we break off in two directions, he says in a serious voice, "You cannot let them keep mistreating you."

He's referring to my aunt and uncle. They don't allow me to use the telephone. If someone phones me, one of them will say, "Julie is busy. Please do not call again."

And when I use the phone, they stand beside me in the kitchen and listen to every word. If I speak Putonghua, they scold me for not practising English. I can never please them. When I won the scholarship from the Toronto Beijing Association, Aunt declared loudly, "You see, we were correct. We made you study hard, and now you see the results."

I'll be very happy when I go away to university in the fall.

In the meantime, I have a cellphone that Aunt and Uncle don't know about. I turn the ring tone off before entering the house. I never forget. At night, I hide it under my pillow. I take it to the bathroom because Aunt checks my knapsack and handbag whenever she can. Good thing my desk faces the door and the mirror that hangs there alerts me when the door opens. While doing homework, I play music on my iPod. Aunt can't tell the difference between iPod earphones and cellphone earphones.

Aunt and Uncle want me to stay at home, but I go to the library on weekends.

"Isn't it quieter here?" Aunt asks.

I tell her I need reference books. I say there are group projects. But Aunt hates those because she's afraid I will help other students get better marks. When I am at school, Aunt searches my room for drugs, make-up, tight clothes—for any sign that I might be breaking her rules.

•

At lunch, Shelley gives me the pregnancy test kit. I go to the washroom, dip the tape into my pee sample, then sit and wait. A cold chill runs up my back, down my arms and into every finger. Shelley says two weeks have to pass after sex in order for the results to be accurate. It's been fifteen days since Eric and I did it.

He's my lab partner in chemistry class. We usually write up our lab results over lunch in the cafeteria. But two weeks ago, Eric said, "Let's do this at a noodle house instead."

The idea of breaking one of Aunt's rules instantly appealed to me. Eric drives his mother's old car, so we went to Lotus Plaza. It has a Chinese supermarket and several Chinese restaurants and noodle houses. The stores there sell women's clothes, pets, art supplies and jewellery. The noodle shop people greeted Eric loudly and happily. We ordered, and he handed me his lab book. Measuring acid strength through solution conductivity was a snap, but writing the results in English sentences was the tough part. When I opened the lab book, I saw a photograph of a dog with a long pink tongue.

"Yours?" I asked.

"My father's."

"What's it called?"

"Teddy."

"It looks like a teddy bear!" I exclaimed. "So lovable."

"When my father immigrated to Canada, my mother and I were still in China. So he bought this dog for company, and whenever they went for a walk, strangers would say hello, ask about Teddy and stroke his fur. It was a good way for him to learn English and make new friends."

"You're so lucky," I said, "to have both your parents here."

He shrugged. "Sometimes it's great; sometimes it's not."

"Who does Teddy love the most?"

"My father, of course."

"And then?"

"Then me. My mother is terrified of dogs."

"If I had a dog, I'd want to take it with me to school every day." I looked adoringly at the photograph. "Teddy is so lovable."

"Come over and meet him." Eric dropped his chopsticks and wiped his mouth. "We've got just enough time before our next class. Teddy loves it when I come home in the middle of the day."

•

Shelley knocks on the toilet door. "What's going on? You should know by now!"

I look down at the test tape and thank God it's negative.

"I told you so," Shelley says. "I can tell with one glance when someone is pregnant. Her face changes; it starts to glow."

As I wash my hands, Shelley nudges me. "Now tell me who it was!"

I shake my head.

"Eric Wu, right?"

I smile and shrug. "No."

"I'll go ask him!"

"Go ahead!"

"It's Benson Li then."

"No."

"Right, he was last year."

I can't tell Shelley, even though she's my best friend. If Aunt should ever find out, she'll send me back to China.

•

At home, I do my English assignment. It's a character study of the Commander, the husband who has sex with the handmaid. At first I hated him. He was a part of the system that oppressed women. But later he broke the rules. He stopped treating the handmaid as just a baby-machine. He played Scrabble with her and gave her magazines to read. He even kissed her. I began to like him and hated his wife, Serena Joy. I began to hope that the handmaid and the Commander would fall in love. I wonder if reading this novel made me have sex. I flip through the novel looking for examples to support my ideas. I should have borrowed Shelley's version because it's easier for me to find key words in Chinese.

There is a knock on my door, and Uncle peers in. I used to address him in Chinese, but then Aunt made a rule that I could only speak English at home.

"Julie, I must warn you." Uncle takes off his thick eyeglasses and wipes his eyes. "Your Aunt will be home soon, and she is in a bad mood."

I hastily look at the shelf where Da-bing, my big stuffed penguin, sits. A while ago, I cut a slit under his left wing and stuffed my cell phone into the slit.

I wish Uncle would tell me more, but he's afraid to take my side. When I first arrived here, I complained about Aunt and Uncle to my father. But Ba said, "After your cousin died, your uncle went crazy for a while. Do not bother him."

Uncle was a professor of English literature visiting on an exchange when he was offered a job here. He never returned to China. Later he sent for his wife and son, De-cheng, who was five years older than me. I remember saying goodbye to him at Beijing airport. When I was eleven, he died in a car accident. Soon afterwards, Aunt sent money to China for Ba to put me into a school with good English teachers. Then Ba announced I would go to Canada to study and live with Aunt and Uncle. I cried, but he insisted I was lucky. Many families wanted an opportunity like this but could not afford it.

I have to respect Aunt. She earns more money than Uncle. She is not beautiful, but she is a beauty consultant. She gives facials and manicures to rich women and advises them on skin care. Her hair is nicely styled, but mine hangs straight. She wears make-up and dresses very well, but she won't allow me to. In the mornings, I leave the house looking like a big sack. I wear baggy sweatshirts and loose jeans. Once, when I went and bought better clothes for myself, Aunt took them away.

"You are here to study," she declared, "not to parade in a beauty pageant."

She intercepts my mail, so Father sends me money at Shelley's address. I buy the clothes I like, but I leave them at Shelley's house. She brings them to school, and I change in the washroom before going to homeroom. If Aunt ever learns about my secrets, she'll be furious. She'll send me back to China, and that will deeply shame Father. People say there is lots of freedom here. Too bad I haven't seen much of it.

Aunt bursts in without knocking. When she is angry, she breaks her own rule and speaks in Putonghua.

"I went to see Mrs. Meng today. You remember her, don't you? She remembers you, because she told me something very interesting."

I wish I could pretend I didn't understand her. She stands at my desk and glares down at me. I know better than to stand up.

"Two weeks ago, she saw you eating noodles at Lotus Plaza. On a weekday. At lunchtime. Is that true?"

I nod.

"Were you alone?"

I shake my head. There is no point in lying if Mrs. Meng saw me. When I breathe, the sweet smell of Aunt's perfume overwhelms me.

"Who were you with?"

"Classmate."

"Boy or girl?"

"Boy."

"Do I know him?"

"I don't know."

"What's his name?"

I shake my head. I won't tell her. "Nothing happened. We went back to school right away."

She raises one darkly painted eyebrow. "When your report card arrives, I'll check your attendance."

At the door, she stops. "If I learn his name, I'll speak to his parents."

I breathe again. If she talks to Eric's parents, he'll never want to see me again.

I reach for my penguin to get my cell and warn Eric, but Aunt bursts back in. "Tried the dress yet?"

I nod.

"Like it?"

I nod, and then she leaves me alone. It's the ugliest dress in the world. She bought it for the scholarship award ceremony. I have no choice but to wear it when I go.

In math class, Mr. Ord gives us a worksheet on factoring polynomials. Then he sits back in his reclining chair with a pleased look. I like factoring because breaking down numbers into their basic parts has a simple logic that reminds me of Lego. Suddenly Mr. Ord calls out, "Hey, listen up. Here's a quickie problem for you bright ones. What do the numbers 3, 7, 8, 40, 50 and 60 have in common? It's something that no other numbers have. I'll give you a minute to tell me."

He repeats the numbers, and I write them down. *Can I beat Hu-lan Xie, the math genius, this time? Are they prime numbers? No, eight isn't. It must be about relationships. Are they part of a series?* I look for patterns, backwards and forwards. I look for combinations. I try addition, subtraction, division, multiplication.

"Time's up!" Mr. Ord grins and peers at the class from his half-lens glasses. "Any takers?"

When there is no answer, he says, "What do those six numbers have in common? They're each spelled with five letters."

A chorus of boos breaks out.

Lincoln Wen, the troublemaker, calls out, "I knew that, sir!"

A few people laugh.

I'm furious. "That is not a math problem, sir," I say.

"Five is a number, isn't it?" he answers.

I go back to factoring again. Teachers here like to play tricks. Westerners find this cool, but I don't.

"Math is about thinking!" crows Mr. Ord. He always has the last word.

•

At lunch, Eric invites me for noodles again, but I refuse. I'm afraid that Aunt might chase us down. In my mind, I see her parked at the Lotus Plaza, watching everyone who enters the noodle shop. She has a heavy pair of binoculars in her gloved hands. Instead, I give Eric an apple, and we sit on the floor outside the biology lab. The deadline for our English essays is Monday, and he still hasn't even chosen a topic. I tell him he should just pick one of Ms. Sandhu's themes.

"Which one is the easiest?"

"You have to find out what the novel is about."

"There's no time."

"Then go to the Internet. There are chapter summaries posted. It won't take you more than ten minutes to read."

"Can't you just tell me which theme is the strongest?" He gives me a pleading look. I don't have the heart to refuse.

The choices are (a) fear is power, (b) the biological need for reproduction, (c) knowledge is power, (d) a woman's strength or (e) hope amidst despair.

I tell him to write about "knowledge is power," and mark the pages that he should read. He'll probably finish writing his essay before me, even get a better score. No he won't, unless I check his grammar.

"Julie, you're wonderful!" he exclaims.

I lean my head against the locker and feel the cold steel against my skull.

"How is Teddy?"

"He's fine. He misses you!"

"Liar!"

"No, really it's true. When I come home, he runs to me and sniffs me like this." His nose touches my neck, and my skin tingles. "He loves your smell."

"When will I get to see him again?"

"Any time you want."

"How about now?"

His face widens into a smile. "Sure! Let's go."

•

Next day, I look forward to seeing Eric. But he rushes off after English class. I am with Shelley, so I can't chase after him. At lunch, I see him with his friends. He is about to head out the main entrance.

"Your English essay, how's it going?" I ask.

Eric looks at his feet before he looks at me. As soon as I see his face, I know there is trouble.

"Your aunt phoned my father yesterday," he says. "She complained that I was a bad influence on you. She told him he should learn to be a better father. She said she's thinking of talking to the principal."

My stomach clenches tight. Eric continues. "When my mother came home from work, my father yelled at her, saying that she wasn't watching over me properly. Now he thinks my marks aren't good enough. My mother is afraid your aunt is going to tell everyone that they are terrible parents. She wants me to stay away from you."

I begin to cry, even though I don't want to.

"I can't stand it when my parents scream and shout at each other."

He runs after his friends.

I vow to never speak to Aunt again as long as I live.

Before, I felt sorry for her. One time, I lost a noisy argument to her. It was about the school ski trip to Quebec. Uncle entered my room as I was sobbing. He patted my back stiffly.

"Don't cry," he said. "Your aunt just wants to protect you."

"I don't need her protection!"

"She thinks this is for your own good."

"Mother would let me go!"

Uncle sighed and sat down beside me. "Your aunt is afraid to fail as a mother, that's why she is so stern."

"She hates me."

"No, she doesn't. She loves you. She loves you as much as she loved our son."

I looked up at Uncle. They never spoke about De-cheng.

"Do you know how De-cheng died?" he asked.

"Accident."

"Terrible car accident. He was racing another car, and your aunt blamed herself. She said she had given him too much freedom."

"But I am not De-cheng."

"Your aunt is afraid that something bad might also happen to you. How would she explain herself to your father then?"

•

To my surprise, this year's scholarship banquet is downtown at the Four Seasons Hotel, in fancy Yorkville, across from the Royal Ontario Museum. The Toronto Beijing Association has grown since I arrived. Three years ago, this event took place in a school gymnasium. Last year it was at a Chinese restaurant. Tonight there are forty tables, all decorated with flowers. I have decided to smile and be polite to everyone. Aunt spent the entire afternoon doing my hair and applying make-up. I look very glamorous, like a movie star. Too bad my dress is so hideous. The material is cream-coloured and heavy, an old lady's choice. The sleeves are puffy and make me look fat. The dress hangs to the ground like window drapes. I still refuse to talk to Aunt.

Instead, I go and chat to Xie Han-ming and his parents. He won the association's athletic award. I'm surprised that Hu-lan, his sister, didn't get one of the scholarships. Her English marks must have pulled down her average. Shelley says Han-ming is gay, but I don't believe her.

Our table has a Toronto city councillor and his wife, and a federal senator and her husband. They all enjoy talking to Uncle because he knows about books and writers and because he has an interesting job. He translates magazine articles and government press releases from English to Chinese for a newspaper. He's well-informed about local and national politics and always surprises people who think that because he speaks English with an accent, he doesn't know very much.

The senator is very smooth. She owns a software company and has two grown children. She doesn't eat much but asks a lot of questions about the Chinese community.

"Are there problems with immigration procedures?"

"Do people register to vote?"

"Is it hard for newcomers to find work?"

"What kinds of help do immigrants expect from the government?"

She knows the city councillor, and they laugh at jokes that no one else understands. Later, she congratulates me on winning one of the scholarships.

"How long have you been here?"

"Which university do you want to attend?"

"What do you want to study?"

She is impressed that I am going to Western to study engineering. She assumes Aunt and Uncle are my parents, but I explain that my real father is back in China.

During dessert, the speeches start. I excuse myself from the table and go to the coat-check room, where Shelley has left a package for me. Then I visit the washroom. When I return to the hall, everyone is listening to the senator from my table. She's at the microphone on stage. In a clear, strong voice, she praises her hosts for working on behalf of the Mainland Chinese community. She says that investing in scholarships is very worthy. There are three scholarships. The first two winners are boys. When my name is called, I stand up and let my shawl fall from my shoulders.

READING THIS NOVEL MADE ME HAVE SEX

As I walk to the stage, I hear people applauding. I look totally different from when I arrived. Shelley lent me a pair of high-heels, so I'm taller. I also borrowed her newest party dress. It's pale blue; the fabric is light and shimmers, and the hem dances above the knees. The dress reveals my bare back, shoulders and arms. I'm also wearing her jewellery. Bands of tiny gems wrap around my wrist and hang from my neck. I confidently walk onto the stage and into the spotlight. I've practised wearing these shoes, so I do not stumble. I shake hands with the president and accept the envelope with my cheque. We stand together for official photographs. Then I go back to my seat.

When the speeches end, everyone stands up to applaud. The city councillor comes over and shakes my hand. The senator says goodbye. A team from the local Chinese TV station rushes over with lights and a camera. I did not expect this. A woman reporter asks me questions in Putonghua. Aunt and Uncle stand stiffly beside me. Then the reporter says with a smile, "Julie, not only did you win a scholarship, but you are also very beautiful."

"Yes, my aunt is a beauty consultant, so she taught me how to look my best."

"You must be so popular at school. How did you find time to study?"

"My aunt taught me to balance freedom with responsibility."

The reporter and the TV camera shift to Aunt. "You are very modern-thinking, Mrs. Fu."

She is flustered and squints into the lights. "I am very proud of my niece," she finally says. "It is very difficult for Chinese youngsters to come here. They are tempted to try so many new things, and who can blame them? If I had come here when I was Julie's age, my life would be totally different."

The reporter congratulates both of us, and then goes looking for the other two winners.

WHAT HAPPENED
THIS SUMMER

SUTTER RIDGE HIGH, ALSO KNOWN AS SUPER RICH HIGH, IS ON THE
OTHER SIDE OF THE HIGHWAY AND IN A DIFFERENT SCHOOL DISTRICT,
BUT NEWS TRAVELS FAST WHEN BLOOD AND CARS ARE INVOLVED. AND
HERE'S THE LATEST.

There's this girl at Sutter Ridge. Her family is from
China but is doing fine. Her mother is well-known. She
does freelance writing for magazines and newspapers. Her
father flies home from China every few months. The girl is
okay-looking and shy; she's liked by all her teachers; and
she wins first prize at the music conservatory for violin.

When she turns eighteen, the mother finally lets her
get a learner's permit. After doing the $1000 driver's ed
course, she breezes through her road test and gets her
licence. Her father comes home and buys her a sports
car to show he loves her. He only has one condition. He
makes her solemnly promise to obey all the Level One
rules. But when she starts driving to school, wham! Her life
totally changes. She joins the fast crowd; boys notice her;

and soon she has a boyfriend. Her cellphone never stops ringing. She's invited to parties every weekend.

One night, she and her boyfriend go out partying and end up at an industrial park way out somewhere with empty roads. Street race! Tragedy waiting to happen! Word gets around fast, and soon there's a crowd cheering on the cars as they slide in and out of hairpin turns.

Some jerk challenges her boyfriend. He takes her car. The two guys line up, rev their engines, and then they're off. They hit speeds of 150 and higher. Then suddenly one car nudges the other, and both cars careen into the air, wham! They slam into a concrete embankment, and a huge explosion lights up the night sky.

Right away, everyone scatters. Everyone thinks the drivers are dead. The girl is hysterical, and someone drives her home. Later that same night she sneaks out of the house and drives off in her mother's car. Next morning, the Parks people find the car in the parking lot at Scarborough Bluff beach. And a day later, her body floats ashore from Lake Ontario.

At the hospital, the two racers miraculously survive their injuries and recover. As soon as the boyfriend gets released, his entire family moves back to China. All this happens way before anyone is thinking about grad.

I don't pay much attention to this story, but all our parents sure do. They wring their hands and shove the newspaper pictures in our faces. The two cars are crumpled together like scrap metal. This is a perfect opportunity for parents to score points about responsible driving, and they take full advantage. As weeks and months go by, the story finally dies. But then grad happens and our beach party, and the next thing I know that story is back, haunting me like a waking nightmare.

Everyone gets bad dreams that are scary and illogical, but at least they're not real. It might feel like you're actually there, breathing and thinking in the middle of some crazy, awful situation. But then you wake up, and you gulp with relief and mutter, *Thank God it was only a dream*. And by the time you eat breakfast, you've almost forgotten it. But for me, that day at our grad beach party keeps haunting me because I lived my nightmare. That's what happened this summer.

•

That day high school is over for good. It's mid-July, hot and sticky on the beach even as the sun begins to drop. We're playing volleyball. I serve and send the ball soaring over the net. Sherman tries to set me up for a slam, but the ball goes high and out. Next I tap one to Jeffrey Jerk, our beloved yearbook editor, but he ends up face down in the sand. I don't bother serving to the girls, because that would make winning the game way too easy.

I look around for Andy, who used to be my best friend. I don't see him anywhere, and it's almost time for the barbecue. I'm in the mood for some serious competition, and the other side needs Andy to make this a decent game. I want him here so that I can show him up. I want to smash the ball over the net into his nose and break it. The more blood the better.

Andy is probably with Crystal Yeh. I called him an idiot for chasing her, because she was Robert Sung's girl. But the next thing we know, Robert Sung dumps her, and Andy and Crystal are hot and heavy, necking in the hallway, cuddling in the cafeteria. They're like glued together. Andy and I, we used to go running, go boarding or go watch movies on weekends. But he stops calling me. I'm out of his life, a total loser. But he couldn't care less. Andy was so happy he was somersaulting in heaven.

I serve again, and this time the losers on the other side manage a spike. My side can't dig it out, even though we should have.

I expected Andy to ask Crystal to set me up with one of her girlfriends, but no such luck. That's the thanks I got for helping him get on the volleyball team. I even let him train on my Bowflex.

I call their serve and set it up for Julia, who dinks it over the net. It isn't elegant, but we get the serve back. Then, mercifully, we win the game.

When I go for my towel, there's a new face under the giant umbrella. She's looking for her bag among the mountain of backpacks. Right away I go to PFI mode. That's Positive First Impression.

"Hi!" I say, smiling. "I'm Wayne. Wayne Lin."

"I'm Esprit," she replies. She squeezes sunscreen onto her arm.

I pretend to reach for a bag so I can lean in close to her. She is sexy with a great body. "Esprit? That's an unusual name."

"It's French," she says.

"Need help with the sunscreen?"

She flashes me a knowing smile that says, *Nice try. Better luck in your next life.* Then she's gone.

"Let's hit the water!" Jeffrey yells, yanking his tee-shirt off and racing down the beach.

The lake is cool, and I swim hard and far out. Most of the kids stay close to shore, but I dive under Julia and grab her legs. She screams and disappears under the water. We grapple briefly and chase one another. It's pure heaven to touch her skin. Somehow the volleyball lands in the water, and a game of dodge ball gets started. Whenever I snag the ball, I aim it at Esprit, but she always ducks away from my shots.

When we go ashore, I see Crystal coming down the path from the parking lot. I run toward her, expecting to see Andy close by. But some older guy comes jogging down the path and grabs her hand. I head for the pile of backpacks, dig out my cell and call Andy. Drops of water fall onto the keypad. I flick them off. Andy isn't answering.

"This is Wayne," I say to his machine, "down at the beach. Listen, Crystal just showed up with some other guy. Maybe you're cool with that. If not, then you better get over here, fast."

I find out that the other guy is Clarence Shou, a second-year-university student. He's tall and has a nice tan. Trust Crystal to clobber Andy with someone who shows that she has rocketed way above our school crowd. She's at a totally different level now.

"This is Wayne," Crystal says. "Wayne, this is Clarence."

She catches me by surprise, and I wonder what game she's playing.

"Good to meet you," he says.

"Wayne was captain of our volleyball team," she adds. "They were district champs."

My face is flattened and reflected on his three-hundred-dollar Oakleys. "Hi there," I say, feeling totally dumb.

They stand there, arms around each other, smiling at me. *What should I do? Fall onto my knees and bow?*

I have to say something. "Uh, so, where'd you get the sunglasses?"

Good grief. Shopping talk.

"New York," says Crystal.

"New York? When did you go?"

"Hey Crystal," booms a familiar voice. "Good to see you."

It's Andy. He cuts in and kisses her on both cheeks. "How've you been?"

"Great," she coos. "This is Clarence. Clarence, Andy."

"Hey Andy," he says. "Good to meet you. Crystal mentioned your name a couple of times."

"Yeah, calling me evil, right?"

"No, she said you were a great guy. You took care of her at grad."

"Yup, that was me." Then Andy turns to me. "Hey, Wayne, old buddy. How've you been? I got your message. Thanks for phoning."

Before I can say a word, he's moved on, and other people are greeting Crystal and Clarence. I go to the clubhouse to take a shower and scrub off the lake's toxic waste. The tap water is lukewarm. I even rinse out my trunks before putting them back on. I see my face in the mirror in the fading light. It's a ripe tomato. No wonder Esprit was scared off.

Back at the party, people are lounging on their towels, taking it easy as the boom box bangs out Radiohead. Lo and behold, what do I see? Andy is teaching volleyball to Esprit.

"Put your left food forward," he says. "You're right-handed, right? Now watch me. Hold the ball at waist level. Let the ball drop, and then swing through. Take it nice and easy."

The ball arches low over the net, and someone tosses it back. "You try it," Andy says. "No! Don't toss the ball. Just let it drop. Try again."

He's right up against her, touching her and getting her into the right position. I watch them, and then I don't want to watch them. But I can't take my eyes off them.

Julia nudges me. "Hey, Captain Wayne. Why aren't *you* coaching her?"

"Who is that girl, anyway?" I nudge her back.

"Must be a friend of Jeffrey's. I think she's from Sutter Ridge."

Jeffrey knows kids from other schools because all the district yearbook teams trained with the printer's resource guy.

Andy is showing Esprit how to set. Her arms are up, hands at her forehead. "Make a triangle between your hands," he says, "like this."

He ducks and comes up in front of her so that his back touches her breasts. "Great," he says. "What you want to do is watch the ball come at you through the triangle."

"I can't do this," she sputters. She slips, falls backwards and bursts out laughing.

I can't take this anymore. I go to the backpack pile and fish around for my sandals. I want to get out of here.

"Hey, where're you going?" Andy asks.

I point to my face. "I need some cream. I'm burning up."

"I'll come with you."

If he does, I'll never get out of here. I've had enough of this stupid scene. "But you just got here."

"Can't stand the sight of Crystal with that guy," he mutters.

"Okay, let's go."

The path up from the beach is loose sand that shifts with each step we take. I wait for Andy to say something. An apology would be nice, for cutting me out of his life for the last four months.

I reach the top first and watch him clamber over the edge.

"So what happened with Crystal?" I ask.

"She says we're better off good friends. Where's your car?"

I can't tell if he's hurting or not. "So she dumped you, eh?"

"You never thought it would work."

I won't deny it. "When did Clarence show up?"

"He was around even when she was with Robert."

Poor Andy. "She really jerked you around, didn't she?"

He slams his door on the passenger side. "Ah, I'm over it. No big deal. Did you see that new girl? She likes me, but I'm not interested in her. I just wanted Crystal to see us together."

This really sucks. Reluctantly, I start the engine and drive out of the parking lot. "That new chick, she's hot," I say.

He stares out his window. "So how's your summer job?"

But all the way to the drugstore he talks about himself and Crystal. I don't want to hear about any of this. I want to know what the hell is going on between *us*. I want to know if we're still friends.

I buy some Noxzema and we head back to the beach. The barbecue is fired up, and there are burgers and sausages and drinks and dope. There are plastic jugs of fruit punch spiked with gin and vodka. It goes down easier than chocolate milk. Jeffrey is passing around some Hawaiian pot. I take a few puffs to relax, because Andy is with Esprit again. I sit by the boom box where it's too loud to talk and let the sight of dancing bodies float me away.

I must have fallen asleep, because the next thing I remember is a full moon above the horizon. Its light cuts a silvery path across the darkened water, right up to our little gathering. A nearby campfire sputters and crackles with sparks rising into the sky. Someone is strumming a guitar. It is so mellow it's like I'm on another planet where time doesn't matter, where everything is cool. But I'm cold and throw a towel around my shoulders. I need to pee, so I stagger to my feet and make my way to the clubhouse. The sand is still warm.

The clubhouse has no electricity, but there's enough moonlight to see. When I reach the door, I hear Andy's voice.

"Is that you, Wayne, old buddy? I've been looking for you."

What the hell does he need me for?

"I gotta get home. I just threw up."

He's not lying. The sour smell of vomit hangs on his breath. I've seen this movie before—Wayne to the rescue.

"I told Esprit I would give her a ride home," Andy says. "But I can't, not like this. I feel like I'm going to puke again. Can you take her?"

What a jerk! "No way!"

"Thanks, old buddy," he says sarcastically and leaves.

I fill the grubby basin with water and plunge my face in to jumpstart my brain. *Maybe I* should *take them home. He's way too wasted.* So I head down to the campfire and ask if anyone's seen Andy and Esprit.

"He's taken her home already," someone mumbles.

"He's one lucky dude," Sherman adds.

"He's too drunk to score," Julia laughs.

"He's too drunk to drive!" I say, and turn and run to the parking lot just in time to see the two of them drive off.

I don't remember driving home, but the next morning my sister wakes the entire house, banging on my door and screaming "Phone!" at the top of her lungs.

I'm so whacked out when I first pick up, I can't figure out who is calling. Then it finally sinks in.

"It's Julia Teng." She takes a deep breath. She sounds scared and tense. "There was an accident last night near the highway. Two cars were totalled. One was Andy's. He didn't make it."

I go totally blank.

"Are you there, Wayne? Wayne, talk to me! Are you there, Wayne? Wayne, talk to me."

Finally, I ask, "What about Esprit?"

"She wasn't with him."

•

The funeral is a week later. All the kids from our class show up. They take it really hard. There's no mention of Esprit at all. People spin off into their own worlds. Jeffrey stops driving altogether and sells his car. Sherman goes to Taiwan, which was definitely not in his plans. Our chat room fizzles out. When Julia leaves for New York, there are no send-off parties because we can't bear to see one another again. The memories of Andy are way too strong. I hear Crystal stopped seeing Clarence.

Then something creepy starts to happen. Apparently the beach where our party took place was the same beach where, after the street race crash, a jogger found the body of that girl from Sutter Ridge High.

Next thing I know, there's a story going around about these Vietnamese teenagers who are partying at the Scarborough Bluff beach when a girl from Sutter Ridge High suddenly joins them. She's friendly and outgoing and flirts with the guys. Everyone is drinking and smoking dope. They pump up the music, dance and make out. When the party ends, a boy offers to drive the girl home. Everything seems cool until the next morning when the kids hear their friend was killed in a car crash. But there's no trace of the girl, and the story keeps on spreading. I hear other versions where the kids are Singaporean Chinese, Malaysian Chinese, Korean or Filipino, but the girl is always from Sutter Ridge High and she always survives.

This is way too strange. Kids make Andy into some kind of ghost story that belongs in the movies or on TV. But I saw that girl Esprit in the flesh. She was real. I remember the warmth rising off her skin. And the other kids saw her too. So why doesn't anyone know what happened to her? I saw her drive off in Andy's car. So why wasn't her body found? Why didn't she show up at his funeral? And why hasn't anyone seen or heard of her since?

Now parents are telling these stories and using them to scare us, because they dread it when we go for a drive. They think for sure we're going to slam into some cute little kid or kill ourselves. They imagine sirens, flashing lights, ambulances, hospitals and bad news. But I get ticked off when kids go around repeating that story. Andy's story is *real*, and it's *my* fault that he's dead. He was *my* friend, and I let him down. I'm not going to let his death turn into a phoney ghost story that kids tell each other for laughs or parents use to lecture us. That's why I wrote this down. That's what happened this summer.

Paul Yee researched eight contemporary Chinese communities across Canada for his book *Chinatown* (2005), while his *Saltwater City*, the history of the Chinese in Vancouver, was recently updated to cover the years to 2001. Among his many books for young readers are *The Bone Collector's Son* (finalist, Vancouver Book Award, 2004) and *Bamboo* (finalist, BC Book Prize, 2006).